To all loves, lost and found.

Chasing Beautiful

(Chasing Series Book #1)

Pamela Ann

Chasing Beautiful
Pamela Ann

Copyright © 2013 Pamela Ann

This is a work of fiction. Names, characters, places, and incidents are either the product of the author's imagination or are used fictitiously, and any resemblance to actual persons, living or dead, business establishments, events or locales is entirely coincidental.

All rights reserved. This book is licensed for your personal enjoyment only. This book may not be re-sold or given away to other people. If you would like to share this book with another person, please purchase an additional copy for each recipient. If you're reading this book and did not purchase it, or it was not purchased for your use only, the please purchase your own copy. Thank you for respecting the hard work of this author.

ISBN: 978-14802263-0-2

Edited by
Alizon and Kristin

Cover design by
Melissa Gill

Interior book design by
Bob Houston eBook Formatting

One

I felt someone's presence before I was fully awake. When I managed to slightly part my eyes, I cursed inwardly from the brightness of the sunshine. *Great, I forgot to close the blinds again last night.*

Willing my sleepy eyes to open a little wider this time, I was stunned to find Blake sitting on my couch, right across from me, wearing a dark scowl. *Why, oh why! Did I give him a spare key, again? Ah, yes! So, that he could have a place to go to if he was feeling out of sorts. What a genius idea that was!*

I rubbed my eyes and yawned loudly. When I finally glanced at his quiet form, he was still wearing a deep scowl on his face, and still not voicing a word.

Okay... "Good morning to you, too," I said with a sleepy voice that dripped with sarcasm. *What's with the attitude?* I added inwardly.

"What the bloody hell were you thinking, Sienna?!" Blake's voice was grating and condescending, his beautifully expressive eyes—midnight blue rimmed with grey and flecks of gold in the middle—flashed with barely suppressed anger; stormy and formidable.

"Excuse me? What in the world are you yapping about, Blake?" His tone took me aback, I definitely wasn't expecting it. Was he drunk, high or something? He didn't look it, but still, that was beyond strange behavior. "Care to *enlighten* me?" I asked, exasperated and annoyed.

I felt like someone had run me over; I probably looked it, too. *I'd give anything for coffee right now*, I sighed at the thought.

What kind of mess was I in? I didn't recall stepping on anyone's toes before I left London to go home, *I think*. I just landed yesterday, jet-lagged and a little drained from my conversation with Luce before she left for Turkey with Toby. *And now this...*

Blake had barged in here like he owned the place with a demanding and taxing demeanor. *Wait, hold on. How did he know I'd arrived already?* Ah, Lucy Connelly probably did the courtesy. She's my friend, my flat mate, and dating Toby Watson—Blake's best friend since childhood. I met Lucy at a college party. She was sweet and genuine, we'd hit it right off. She casually mentioned that the woman who she shared an apartment with left for New York to follow her boyfriend. So I'd immediately inquired about the vacant room.

I was living in student housing then, but needed my own place—away from cat-fights, drunken noise and drama. She offered excitedly and wanted me to check it out the next day. I moved in two days later and our friendship blossomed to the point where we became each other's closest confidant.

She went to school with Toby and Blake at the London School of Economics. When she started dating Toby, two weeks after I moved in, I became friends with the two men; more so with Blake, though. We'd just clicked. That was a little over eight months ago.

"I ran into Lucy last night in Toby's flat, and she casually mentioned that you came back, without telling anyone, might I add. So, OBVIOUSLY, I wanted to visit you, but she stopped me, revealed that you were in a delicate state. So, of course, my curiosity was piqued. I badgered her until she told me what she knew and learned about your *'little interlude'* with Kyle, *while his girlfriend was on the premise.* I believe that the intention of 'closure,' indeed, was lost on you." Blake's furious expression deepened when he said 'little incident.' *Oh, shit.*

I blushed.

Shit-fuck-shit.

He probably thinks I'm a hussy now, giving in to Kyle's advances.

I glanced away from him quickly. *Is he ticked off that I haven't called him about what happened and instead, learned it from Lucy?* He even managed to sound hurt?

I'm sort of in a tricky situation; Kyle cheated on his girlfriend—with me. When I told Luce, she was shocked and felt wretched for me. So, it was no surprise really that Blake was angry.

"Yeah, about that... it was merely a moment of madness—I'm shattered about it. I mean, who wouldn't be in my situation? My emotions got the best of me," I said lamely. Or maybe I was just plain horny and had made a beeline for it!

I wanted to erase the whole entire visit back home from my lagging memory.

"How could you put yourself in that position? I didn't understand the bloody need to go and get 'closure'. He already started seeing someone else before he called to break it off with you. *Have you forgotten about that?* He's a cheater! Yet you still went prancing back to Los Angeles, and to make matters worse, he took advantage of that. You were intoxicated and placed yourself in *danger!*" His scowl deepened. "You could've been hurt, Sienna."

I was, not in the way he was implying, but my heart and pride were crushed. "Good God. I was in no way or shape in any danger. You seriously exaggerate and blow things out of proportion! Really now, Blake... it's Kyle we're talking about here. He would never hurt me, not like that." I fidgeted with my lemon chiffon-colored, six hundred count sheets, trying to gather ground.

Was it really pathetic to look for closure? No, but if the guy in question had cheated, surely closure is out of the question? My thoughts queried.

Blake sighed deeply and got up from the couch, standing in front of me, holding out his hand. His frame dominated the room. It was a pretty decent size, but put Blake's presence anywhere and the result would be the same; size be damned. He had that pulling power around him and his dark good looks just enhanced it.

He was dressed in nude chino shorts, a blue dress shirt that was pushed back to his elbows and tan, soft-leather loafers. He looked like he had just stepped out of a Dolce & Gabbana summer photo shoot. Sometimes I wish he was average looking; then it would be easier to look at him without melting.

A few strands of his wavy locks fell onto his forehead. Looking down at me, his beautiful face was complacent. "I made the courtesy of brewing some coffee. Come, you look like you need some." *Oh, don't I just.* I took his outstretched hand and he pulled me out of bed. "I was worried, Sienna. I care for your well-being. Don't be cross." I looked down, not meeting his gaze.

The man towered over my five-foot-two stature. Blake inhaled deeply, smelling my forehead before kissing it then he grabbed my hand and we walked towards the kitchen where the smell of freshly brewed coffee emanated, drawing me closer.

He didn't utter another word until I'd had my first sip of caffeine. "How are you really feeling? Okay? Not okay?" Blake was studying my reaction, pensive.

"Yes—no—*I don't know?* Can one ever be okay after a broken heart?" I shrugged. "I'm sure I'll move on, but I doubt I'll put my heart out there like that again. It was traumatizing enough doing it once. Being vulnerable is something I don't take lightly—with my background and all." I sipped my scalding coffee without batting an eyelash. It was true; vulnerability reminded me of my demoralizing childhood and Hell would freeze over before I put myself in that compromising position again.

Blake's handsome head nodded in agreement with evident understanding. He had an idea of my rotten years of misery, but had never really pushed me to talk about it. I appreciated it and respected him for it.

Both of our parents died when we were young and it was something we have in common. It gives us a platform of understanding. A place where we don't have to explain, but we simply understand the pain, the loss, the daunting uncertainty of loneliness and the frightening feeling of what looms on the horizon.

Blake and I immediately became close after Lucy started dating Toby. We liked the same books, shows, board games, amongst other things. We hit it off right off the bat and hung out once a week or so when he wasn't busy with his women, and there'd been a lot.

In the beginning, both Luce and Toby thought we would start dating, too, but after a few months of insinuating, they finally let-up—accepting the fact that we clearly *were* just friends, platonic friends. I must admit that, at times, my mind drifts off and I imagine what it would be like to date someone like Blake. Six-foot-three, all muscles and the most arresting face; full lips, straight nose, chiseled jaw and his unique eyes were hypnotizing.

Sometimes I got caught up staring into those eyes and forgot where I was. Blake was the sexiest man—sinfully beautiful—my eyes had ever graced. I always snapped myself back to reality when I reminded myself that he was only a good friend and he dated tall, beautiful, leggy, statuesque women; preferably lingerie models. My Coca-Cola-bottle-shaped form did not stand a chance. Sure, most red-blooded males find me desirable and gorgeous, but with Blake, I simply felt Plain Jane.

"...so it should be okay, right?" I wasn't paying attention to what he was saying and my dumbfounded look seemed to annoy him. Glaring at me and combing his hair with his right hand, he looked frustrated. Something was bugging him. "Sienna... I was asking you if you wanted to eat breakfast."

"You haven't had breakfast yet? How come? You never leave anywhere without eating first thing in the morning..." I trailed off. "Hold on, how long have you been here, sitting and scowling at me like a bear with a sore head?!" My accusing green-gold eyes held onto his midnight silver blue.

"Awhile..." I glared at him some more, not budging. "Okay, okay. I think... quite possibly around four in the morning, I suppose?" He looked sheepish admitting that and he started to run his fingers through his dark locks, again. That habit comes out when he's anxious. He didn't know that I know that, but I've noticed it enough. I notice everything about him.

Did I hear that right? He's been here since four in the morning? "WHAT!?!"*Oh, hell.* He was really pushing it. People break-up and get hurt all the time. There was no need to go to such lengths on my account.

"I was concerned about you. I was worried and wanted to see for myself that you were okay. You're one of my closest friends, Sienna. Sometimes, even more than Toby; I didn't want some bloody, idiotic wanker treating you badly—as though you're worth *nothing*! You weren't picking up your bloody phone so I rushed over—like the good friend that I am—checking if you'd drunk yourself to a stupor or what of it."

"I was sleeping! So obviously, it was on silent!" I snapped at him.

He has a very active imagination. How will he run his granddad's empire if he's extremely paranoid? The whole company will crumble under his thumb in a week! The thought made me smile. That would be a sight to see. Knowing how he was, though, he'd excel and surpass everyone's expectations like he always did.

His frown deepened.

I scowled.

Not able to stand the feeling of being at odds with him, I grabbed his hand and pulled him towards the couch.

Our living room was painted in egg-shell yellow and consisted of two huge couches, a HD television and a coffee table as well as other knick-knacks to make it warm and inviting. The contrast of dark, wooden floor and a huge, baby blue area rug gave it a homey, cozy feel. It was spacious and airy at the same time, never stifling. I loved that flat. I felt like I belonged here.

We sat next to each other on one of the dark, mustard colored couches, touching at our shoulders and thighs. I glanced down and studied the outline of his well-toned, muscular thighs, my eyes full of admiration. Uncomfortable, I looked at my very skimpy, cotton, soft-pink baby doll dress and felt a little flustered.

How the heck did I manage to forget that I'm wearing almost next to nothing? I tried to cover my thighs by pulling it down more, but there was very little fabric to pull.

Get over it, I told myself. Blake won't be interested. Might as well strip naked and test it. He'd probably beg you to get dressed before you embarrassed both of us more. I smirked at the thought.

I tended to push his buttons a lot, much to his dismay.

"Look, Blake, I apologize for my rude behavior. I'm sure if something happened to you, I would do the exact same thing. I was just taken aback. Thank you for caring. It means a lot to me. I suppose I should've seen it coming with Kyle. We hadn't seen each other for nine months and we'd grown apart tremendously. The signs were there, but I ignored them. Somehow, deep down, I might've guessed that it was bound to happen. Kyle was a big part of my past and it's sad that things had to end this way. We could've parted on nicer terms, but it happened and I just have to accept that." That seemed to lighten his mood; just a *tad* bit.

I took his right hand with my left and squeezed it tightly. Holding it, he took his other hand and touched my chin, making me look straight into his eyes, our faces only a few inches apart. I felt my stomach drop and I was mesmerized. *I've never been this close to Blake. WOW! He easily takes my breath away. He's so beautiful! Be still, my heart.*

"Are you sure you're okay? Tell me, honestly? I want to beat his bloody ass to a pulp for hurting you! I warned you about that trip." *Obviously still angry and frustrated, I see.*

Blake was such a good friend, maybe even a best friend. He cared for me. There were only a few that did and I'd treasure them forever. I suddenly felt like I had a lump in my throat.

I cleared my throat and reached out to hug him. "I'm a bit better now, Blake. Don't fuss about me! Sure, it was awful—you know—but the whole ordeal made me look at the bigger picture and I realized that I can't hold on to the past... even if it is something I hold dear to my heart. I have to let it go and move on," I whispered to him as my head nestled on his broad shoulder. I moved a little closer to his neck, wanting to rest my head and fall back to sleep again. He smelled delicious, which was a combination of a hint of lemon aftershave and something masculine.

He smelled divine; I sighed loudly. *How ironic is this? He came here to console me and here I am thinking naughty thoughts about him?*

I hate it when I got this weird feeling with Blake; it happened once in a while and, to be honest, it made me act awkward afterwards. I was a woman and just because he was my friend, it didn't make me immune to his charms or his striking looks. *Or his mouth-watering smell.* GAH!

I released him from my hug and sat back to enjoy my coffee.

Clearly my reaction to his smell bothered me. "Let's get you out. Let's do something fun; after we have breakfast at The Wolseley?" Blake looked like he was trying to conjure a plan.

"Like what?" I thoughtfully asked him, knowing well enough that he didn't quite know what the heck it was. He loved throwing ideas out and acting on them, spontaneous man that he was.

"Whatever you fancy," he said it with purpose as he sat back, splaying both arms on the back of the couch, legs both on the table, resembling a Greek god, lazing about with sheer contentment. His strong, thick, powerful legs were showcased before my lustful eyes.

Is there anything this man is made of that isn't sinful? Everything about him screamed of sin and sex and I was hot and bothered. *Am I always this hyper-aware of Blake? Has it always been like this?* Quite possibly. It was too much; my sleepy state couldn't process the heavy confusion and the coffee seemed to be working weakly.

Hell.

"Knightly, it was your idea. If you ask me, I'd rather sit at home and just sleep some more. Oh! How about we just watch movies here all day on the couch?" I smiled sweetly at him. *Give in, please. I don't want to shower and get dressed*, I thought lazily.

"That would not be a good idea, poppet. Get up, you little skive, and get dressed! I'll have it figured out before we leave, all right?" Blake ordered, giving me his signature killer smile complete with his sexy dimples showing.

I loved it when he called me poppet in that cute, British accent. Truth be told, I had a hard time saying no to him when he dished out *that* type of smile and he bloody well knew it.

I groaned, got up and threw a hap-sack pillow at his head. "This better be worth my time, Knightly." I gave him my I'm-not-so-amused face and started to leave when he suddenly pulled me down next to him on the couch.

"Do you trust me?" Indeed, I did. I nodded and went to my room to get changed.

Why was he being so intense about the whole Kyle thing? It was absolutely uncanny. I wasn't sure if I liked him being that way towards me.

Two

Showered and ready to go, I gave myself a once over in the full-length mirror that hung on my bathroom door. I wore a powder blue, cotton dress that fitted tightly around my torso and flared nicely at the bottom, sitting two inches above my knees. I accented the dress with mustard-colored, wedge espadrilles and hastily placed my naturally wavy, dark hair in a loose bun, evoking simplicity while still achieving a sexy look.

I applied tinted moisturizer, pink gloss and just enough mascara to bring out my bright green eyes with a burst of gold popping out of them. It was one of my best features. Even if I felt like death inside, I needed to look at least presentable. It was part of the coping mechanism I learned when I was ten-years-old—always look put together.

My golden-brown skin could be credited to my Brazilian/Caucasian mixed heritage. Spritzing my signature Coco Mademoiselle, I grabbed my tan Botkier tote and headed towards where Blake was patiently waiting for me.

I found him in the kitchen on the phone. He turned around and gave me a swift examination before ending the call. "Ready?" he politely asked, as he stayed rooted to his spot.

"Yep."

"To breakfast, *milady*." He held out his arm to link with mine.

I smiled stupidly at him as we walked out the door and straight to the elevator. "Figured anything out yet?" I questioned, referring to 'his plan of action'.

"Sorted as promised, but it's a surprise..." He looked impish and smug so I nudged him.

As we emerged from the elevator, we headed towards the main entrance. "You have got to be joking! Why does it have to be a surprise? I *hate* surprises!" I exclaimed. I *did* hate surprises because surprises were horrible, *every* single time. So, I was a tad skeptical about that one.

"You did agree to trust me; remember, poppet?" he asked, gazing at me with a playful smile as the sunshine accentuated his beautifully sculpted features, making him look annoyingly sexy as we hit the sidewalk.

A few women who passed by stared openly at him. A harried woman stopped, halting in her tracks, awed, and just ogled—previous destination long forgotten as she was rooted to the cement sidewalk. Yeah, yeah he was hot. *So, What?* I wanted to snap that woman out of her trance.

Don't get me wrong; I adored Blake. I thought he was smart, articulate, funny, crazy talented and had a heart of gold, which was reserved for those he trusted, but it could be exhausting to be his friend. Lucy had the same problem. We were the only women that Blake was friends with so we were constantly hounded for trivial information. *Anything*, to help them out, they'd say. "Right, if Blake really wanted a woman, he'd pursue her relentlessly, not the other way around," had been the reply out of Lucy's very owns lips.

I go to a Fashion School, majoring in Fashion Marketing, and of course, the women there asked me about him after he picked me up from school once. He was parked on the curb and leaning on his sexy car looking absolutely delicious; that alone drove questions from six—*SIX!*—adult, grown women who had their panties twisted. The girlfriends I brought from school to party with us a few times brought hysterics into the mix at their first glance. Like "OMG, have you SEEN that ASS?" or "HOLY FUCK! He's GORGEOUS!" or "Shit, Sienna, can you hook me up?" There was more, but I don't want to elaborate any longer; it was taxing on my precious sanity. Blake, of course, never hooked-up with any of them because they weren't lingerie model material.

Glancing at him, I shrugged. "Yeah, right," I said, thinking that this surprise better not suck or I was going back to my bed to wallow, sleep and then wallow some more.

Jet-lag, thoughts of Kyle... what else?

Kyle... did he know I'd left home? Home was Los Angeles for me and where Kyle was. My best friend, my protector... my first love, my first everything—before he totally broke my heart almost a month ago when I got *that* call.

Kyle and I had practically grown up together. He lived a few houses down from me. We were each other's strength ever since we were seven years of age and we'd never grown apart, until I left for school in London. After a few months, he started being distant and talked to me over the phone only very reluctantly, and when he did, he was extremely nonchalant. I explained away his attitude with viable reasons such as he missed me or he couldn't stand having me so far away from him and all. I had ignored the warning signs all too easily.

Wanting to bridge the wedge between us, I decided to surprise him. I had a two-week window in between semesters so I could easily visit him, but before I booked the ticket, he called me.

I was the one surprised.

That call had shattered everything that I'd believed Kyle and I had along with my belief that we were invincible. He told me that he'd met someone else and he had been seeing her for a month. He justified his actions by stating that it was too difficult without me there and he was lonely.

Lonely?!

Two years of being together, not to mention that we'd been best friends since the age of seven, thrown out the window because he was *lonely*?! What a cruel joke.

Of course, Luce, Chad and Blake consoled me and all three begged me to forgo my trip to Los Angeles. They'd argued that he wasn't worth it and I might just end up regretting the decision. However, I held my ground and still managed to book that blasted airline ticket.

I wasn't a coward and I needed to see it for myself. To hear him say it—I *needed* him to *tell me* that it was over.

Guiding me to the parked Black One 77 Aston Martin on the curb, Blake opened the door and let me in. The heady perfume of leather and Blake's signature aroma annihilated my nostrils, making my stomach churn; I *love* his smell.

Opening his door, he slid onto the black leather seat next to me, pulled out his aviator shades and started the engine, pulling into traffic towards Piccadilly. Some of his hair fell on the side, looking like a sinfully sleek rock god, in control and dominating.

What's with Italian men and glorious hair, anyway? Even if he was only half Italian—he'd certainly got the coloring and the hair thing going on. I couldn't help my thoughts sometimes. My reaction towards him came naturally. He was simply too damn sexy.

"Did you sleep at all last night?" I asked, looking at him to see his facial expression.

He smirked. "No, not really."

I frowned at his answer. "But... why? You could've confronted me in the morning, Blake. Why the need to show up that *late*?" I was nursing my ego, pride and my heart, but I certainly was not suicidal.

Blake exhaled deeply, his voice dark. "I needed to see with my very own eyes that you were not crying into oblivion or drowning in alcohol. I was worried. It didn't help that you were alone in the flat and I reprimanded Lucy for leaving you in the state that you were in, even if she argued that you wanted to go straight to bed." He looked so serious and started to get angry again.

"It's not Lucy's fault that I showed up unannounced a week earlier than arranged, and besides, they had planned a trip to Turkey. I wasn't about to have her stay back here because I had my heart broken. That's ludicrous! She was worried, but I convinced her to leave me alone. I needed to be left alone last night and I thought, deep down, she knew that it was what I needed." Blake looked pensive and seemed not to buy my argument.

I tugged at his shirt. "Blake, you can't seriously be mad at Lucy. She didn't do anything wrong," I was adamant that he believe me. I wasn't going to let him be mad at Lucy and he knew it, too. He was merely trying to drive me insane. They were my friends and they meant a lot. They'd become like family.

Taking my hand and linking his fingers with mine, he placed both of our hands on his thigh before he spoke. "I hate seeing you hurt, Sienna. You're one of my best friends; I cannot endure you being shattered and vulnerable. You always had this easy going, happy attitude about you, and after you got that call, you've changed. I know you're hurt, poppet, but let me *help* you ease some of the pain? You're not alone in this. If the situation were reversed, you would do exactly the same thing for me. Let me take care of you until you're better."

Surprised and astonished by his speech, I gathered my dumbfounded brain to make a response. *How lucky am I to have a friend like Blake?* He didn't talk much about his family, but from what I had gathered from Toby, to those he let in, he'd be their friend for life. A sort of til-death-do-us-part type of loyalty.

Blake sounded too serious and I needed to lighten up the mood. Quirking my left eyebrow at him I asked, "*Ease* some of my pain, Knightly? Wonder how *easily* you can manage that! Tell me where and when and I'll show up, *milord*." I wore a seductive smile as I batted my lashes at him, going for the full effect. *Yeah, sucker!*

He flashed his magnetic smile as he swiftly parked the car and killed the engine, giving me his undivided attention. "Are we frisky today, my sweet?" he drawled, brushing subtle strokes on my arm that still held his right hand. *Ha, I see how you're going to play this. Two can play that game.*

"¿Cuánto me quieres, *papi*?" *How much do you want me, papi?* I purred at him, knowing full well he spoke fluent Spanish amongst other languages. Papi meant daddy, but it was widely used as an endearment in other Spanish-speaking countries, mostly in a sexual situation.

I leaned over him, inhaling his smell as I whispered seductively, "Te deseo, papi—*dentro* de mí." *I want you, papi—inside me.* Pulling back, I bit my lip and gazed at him through my lashes for the full-effect.

His chiseled jaw dropped while the air crackled, heavy with arousal. I felt him hold my hand tighter. He swallowed hard and groaned. *Okay.* I kind of over did that, but I couldn't help teasing him. I just wanted to see if he would take the bait and he had.

I burst out laughing. I couldn't help it. It was simply too intense; I had to figure out a way to diffuse the weird situation I had gotten myself into. Laughing always seemed to work.

"I'm sorry; I got carried away. I couldn't help teasing you. The opportunity was there and I just had to grab it!" I smiled at him with pure innocence.

He laughed his throaty, sexy laugh, too. "Woman, you almost gave me a heart attack! That was some sexy stuff you just pulled. You're lucky I didn't take the bait and have my wicked way with you!" With a sexy wink, he opened his door to get out of the car.

He went to my side, opened the door and offered his hand to help me out. Chivalry's always alive and kicking with Blake and Toby. I was lucky to have found Lucy as my flat mate and to have made very good friends with those two caring men, Blake especially.

"Did you make a reservation?"

Chasing Beautiful

"Don't worry about anything. I got it handled," Blake said reassuringly. I nodded. I was sure he had. I mean, did men like him need reservations, anyway?

"Mr. Knightly, how lovely it is to see you again. How is your grandfather?" questioned the maître d', a middle-aged man wearing a suit and thick glasses, as he ushered us to our table.

"He's lovely, thank you." Blake responded casually, placing his hand on my back as we headed to our table.

"Here we are! Let me know if there is anything that I can do for you, Mr. Knightly. Good to see you again. Enjoy," he said enthusiastically, looking at Blake and then me.

"Thank you, Gerard." Gerard gave a light nod, smiled towards me and stealthily left our table.

I knew his granddad came here often with him. Blake adored his grandfather. He had taken him in when Blake was ten-years-old, after both of his parents had tragically died in an avalanche in the Swiss Alps while skiing on their wedding anniversary. I met his grandfather, William, once during my visit to Blake's flat in Mayfair when his grandfather decided to give him a surprise visit. He was charming and engaging. From the affectionate way they interacted, I knew they loved each other deeply. I was happy for Blake because, even though tragedy had struck him, he still had a loving family member to care for and support him unconditionally, unlike me.

"I'll have Eggs Benedict and a cappuccino, please." I didn't need to look over the menu. I knew what I wanted.

"A woman with a hearty appetite. I like that." I snorted and laughed. *Ha! I'm sure you do.*

"What's so funny?"

"You."

He raised a brow, curious and waiting. "*And?*"

I shrugged. "It's just—you know—you only date models or ones that look it and I bet those types hardly eat or, if they do, simply nibble at their food. I'm sure," I said sarcastically. *Why does he date only women that look like that?* I hadn't pegged him to be a shallow man, but then again, I supposed his libido made the decisions. I truly was curious and wanted to know the truth, however I didn't have the nerve to actually voice *that* question out loud.

"I do not!"

I shrugged, not wanting to argue.

After the waiter had come and taken our order, Blake had to go outside to take a business call. I was left to my own devices, so I pulled out my phone and texted Jen. I let her know that I had gotten back okay, that she shouldn't worry about me and I would call her as soon as I got a chance. She was a good friend from back home and was one of the people in my support system. She was there with me when I saw Kyle with his new girlfriend. Thinking about that made my stomach churn and burn with acid.

Fuck.

The bitch gave me a smirk and held Kyle's arm, looking at me with a scornful expression. I didn't go back there to steal him from her. I just needed closure, but I'd gotten more than I had bargained for.

Three

Saturday, Santa Monica,

Katie's Beach House Party

(8 days ago)

"What's your choice of poison?" The über hot bartender asked, wearing only surfer shorts and a garter bowtie to complete his ultra-surfer look. Hot might be understated, more like scrumptious. Exotic with caramel eyes and a to-die-for smile accompanied by perfect teeth.

I giggled like a schoolgirl. "Um, I'd like a lemon drop and a..." I trailed off glancing at Jen.

"What would you like to drink, Jen?"

"I'll have sex on the beach, babe," she said with a wink. *I'm sure she just wants that with a little sand and soft waves. Flirt.*

He started setting up our drinks as I pulled Jen next to me. She was still looking at the bartender through her eyelashes and I knew right then and there that she had already set her sights on him.

"Jen, we just got here, *can the flirting wait?* I kind of need you to stick with me tonight. I sort of need armor, or more like a shield," I said with an antsy smile and pleading tone.

"Doll, you can't be seriously hung up on Kyle still, are you?" Jen asked accusingly, her brows furrowed.

"Umm... well, I don't know... I want to talk to him—"

"What do you mean you don't know? He cheated! You *can't* second guess that, sweetie. He's moved on, and from what I've heard, things have been getting steadily serious."

That did sound like a very good point.

Steady and serious. Huh. Wow. *How could he do this to me? To us?*

I wanted to scream and lash out at him, but it wouldn't change what he'd done. I guess he didn't want to wait; he wanted a change. I was hoping to catch him tonight and talk. I didn't try calling his phone because I wanted to see his face. I needed this closure so I could bury the hatchet forever and never look back with regret. I needed a clean slate, no doubts hanging about in my semi-lucid brain.

I knew he was going to show up; he always showed up at parties and I didn't doubt that his ladylove would be with him, too.

"Whatever, it doesn't matter... just hang with me for a bit okay? I promise to take you for fro-yo tomorrow," I said as I avoided her question. I couldn't answer that myself at that moment. That had always been our go-to place; second to Starbucks.

"Here you go, ladies! Enjoy!" purred the *hot-tender*.

"Thanks," we said, synchronized.

"Okay, I'll stick with you for a while, but not long. I don't want someone else snagging that nice piece of meat before I do! God, have you seen that tight body?" Jen delightfully noted, glancing back to the bartender before heading to the beach where some people we knew from high school were located.

"I want to just drag him somewhere dark and see if those lips live up to my imagination! Do you think he'll be into me?"

I glanced at her like she had two horns on her head. "Have you gone mad, hon? You know you're a knockout, right? Besides, he was totally checking you out."

Seriously, sometimes I thought she didn't really know how beautiful she was. That part of Jen was the doing of a stupid, selfish ex-boyfriend who'd mentally and emotionally derided her and she totally succumbed to the douchebag's manipulative ways because she had been blinded by love.

In love or not, a person didn't deserve to be treated like that. That type of abuse could take a long time to recover from. Had I known that in the beginning, I would've snatched her away from Tony. However, for three years she'd never said a word about any of it. From the outside, everything seemed undeniably perfect. Everyone had always thought they were perfect for each other. I did, too. I adored Tony. That's why, when she confessed her dilemma, I took charge and let her stay with me until everything blew over and until Tony realized that she was serious about leaving him. Our senior year, she started to blossom into her own person and had been loving life ever since.

Most men I knew had a hard time resisting Jen when she was on the prowl—there was no chance in hell her chosen man could escape. Who would really want to resist someone who resembled Heidi Klum in the looks department? Apart from Jen having killer looks, she had a sharp mind and she was currently studying at USC to be a lawyer. She'd make a killing out of that one.

"Jen! Sienna! Good of you beautiful ladies to grace us with your presence tonight!"

"Mickey! I've missed you!" I laughed, giving him a huge hug and a peck on the cheek.

Mickey's the kind of guy who was always nice and respectful. He was second generation Samoan and had the size of one, too. He played defense on our football team at Notre Dame High School in Sherman Oaks. You'd never catch him talking crap about other people, though. He had never been that kind of jock. Jen and I adored Mickey, everyone did.

"Nice to see you again, Jen!" Mick gave her a quick bear hug and released her with a grin.

"You, too, Mick." She jokingly punched his arm before she headed towards some other people we used to hang out with. I casually waved at the group and continued to stick with Mick. I didn't want to go over there and hangout. It would just invite questions and gossip about Kyle that I wasn't ready to discuss.

I scanned the area for any sightings of Kyle, but it seemed he had yet to arrive. I looked back at Mickey who seemed to be studying me with a twinkle in his eye.

"Looking for someone in *particular*, Sienna?" *Fishing, I see.*

"Huh? Oh, no. Just taking in the scene and seeing who else I know here. It feels good to be back home again, Mickey! I forgot how beautiful it was out here during summer time."

Indeed, it was a magnificent night. The full moon was up high and bright amidst the darkened sky. It was illuminating the ocean and making it look breathtakingly ethereal, serene and peaceful. The waves lapped softly on the shore and I felt calm inside, wishing Blake was here with me. He would have liked it. My trio of friends had offered to come, but I'd refused them. I needed to do this one on my own.

"How are you?" I asked as I sat on the wooden lounger, glancing back to Mickey and enjoying my cold, alcoholic beverage.

"Actually, a lot has been going on, man. I'm leaving for Alaska next week to help out my dad. He's been feeling exhausted from running the business. So, it's my turn to step-up and help the family," he said solemnly.

"I'm sorry to hear that, Mick. I recall you weren't really fond of that place," I said, empathizing with his situation.

"Damn right, but I got to help the family out, so there's no other option." He took a chug of his Corona, studying the sand on his feet.

There was someone hollering from behind me so I twisted my head to glimpse who the culprit was. Kyle was hugging and high-fiving people along the way. His other right hand was attached to a very attractive blonde who was gazing and smiling lovingly at him.

Perfect. Just bloody, fucking perfect.

I felt awkward and anxious. *Fuck. Should I go over and say hi? Maybe I should play indifferent?* I castigated myself for being idiotic. *Come on, Sienna,* I scolded myself. *Deep breaths and think of something relaxing.*

Crap-fuckity-crap.

"'Kay there, doll?" Jen sat next to me with her arm loosely on my shoulder.

"Course! Should we get more drinks?" *Might as well get some encouragement from my old pal, The Don, Patron.*

"Oooo! Shots?! That should get us going!"

"Hell, yeah!"

"Bring on the happy face, doll. Don't let him see anything else." I nodded, not wanting to say anything else. She was right, of course.

We got up and headed back to the house. I knew we would be passing Kyle at any moment so I willed myself to play it cool and not take it too seriously. *Who cares if we dated two gloriously fun-filled years? Really, who cares?* Uh! I was getting idiotic after only one drink.

"Hey, Jen! *Sienna, you're back,*" greeted a merry-looking Kyle.

"Hey there! Congratulations on your internship! I'm hearing that they'll hire you before you even finish school," Jen playfully said to Kyle. They got on so well back in the day, it was no wonder they were falling back into an easy banter.

Kyle's working with his father now. He loved music. He'd grown up with it, learning everything and anything music related from his father. His dad owned a major record label company here in LA so it was a no brainer that he'd be following in his dad's footsteps. Most importantly, he loved to scour for musicians that had depth and soul in them in order to help them be successful in the music industry. He was quite passionate with his work and I remembered how he used to light up and get all excited when talking about it.

"Ha ha! How I've missed your craziness!" Kyle said with his deep, playful laugh. *God, I've missed that laugh. Here goes my stupid brain.*

I looked like a complete idiot standing there next to Jen while they were catching up. His girlfriend, whom he hadn't introduced yet, was curiously eyeing Jen and me. *Did Kyle talk about me? Is that why she's eyeing me up and down now?* Hah. Bitch.

Kyle turned his attention to me and his laughter died the minute our eyes met. His hazel eyes looked intense and fiery. His face looked calm, but I knew, deep down, he was mad. Damn, he looked gorgeous.

A deep ache settled in my heart. *I miss him.*

His white v-neck shirt outlined his defined torso and arms. *My word, is he more buff and defined or what?* My eyes roved all over him. *Yes, he's been working out.* His body was a lean, muscular type; different from Blake's physique, but still downright sexy.

"How long are you here for? I didn't expect you to be back for your break—would've thought you'd be traveling all over Europe or somewhere much more exotic rather than coming back here to *plain,* old Los Angeles," he said cuttingly with barely hidden bitterness lacing his words.

"Um, I've missed Jen and needed to tie up some loose ends with the conservatorship (outright lie) so, I decided to come back during break. It's only two weeks anyway so I won't be staying long." *Shit, I sound so lame. Couldn't I come up with something better to say?* Sigh.

Why was he being all cold, anyway? He was the one who broke-up with me.

"Right, anyway ladies, I want you to meet my amazing girlfriend, Brooke," he announced as he hooked his left arm around his *amazing* girlfriend. She had a huge, cat-like, fake smile and a massive rack. GAG. She looked fake, an absolute Blonde Bimbo.

She was clingy, giggly and used a whiney voice like a little girl—it made me want to scratch the wall with my nails. I hated her already, and from the look of pure disdain she was giving me, the feeling was mutual. Since when was Kyle attracted to BB's anyways? He'd always made fun of them.

"Hey! Pleasure to meet you people—but we must go and mingle with others. Kyle? I see some of your friends are already in the tub. Let's go! I can't wait to get you wet, baby!" she said coaxingly as she grabbed his hand and left for the tub at lightning speed. Nice, she was amazing indeed.

Not.

Four

"*Nice* girlfriend there," Jen remarked when Kyle and BB walked away.

"Don't mention it. I know you're dying with questions, but let's skip it tonight, okay?" I pleaded.

The house was in full-on grinding, party mode as the speakers pounded, blaring "Birthday Cake" by Rihanna.

"Hey! Why don't you stay put and mingle with the eager men out here, hmm? I'll go get us our drinks, lemon drop or a shot?" Jen suggested. I looked at Jen with a raised eyebrow. I knew she was going to go check out the hot-tender and have her wicked way with him, so I wasn't going to trouble myself by getting in line for drinks.

"How about both, please? I'm in dire need of them." I winked at her as I fished out my phone from my purse and checked for messages.

I got three emails from friends back home—Chad, Blake and from Lucy/Toby.

> From: Lucy Connelly
> Subject: Miss you!
> Be strong and don't forget to enjoy! In case you forgot... you're on vaca, too!
> See you when you get back!
> WE love you,

Lucy and Toby xxxxx

Lucy's message made me smile. She liked to smother people with as much x's as she could in her messages and I loved her for it.

From: Chad Wilson
Subject: Guess What!
Baby girl! You would never guess! I just got a spot on a show! I'm so psyched! Couple of months away, though, but shit! This is crazy! How's vacation? Call me the moment you land on Heathrow!
I miss you, lover!
Your ever sexy java-mamba friend,
C xxx

Oh, Chad! I'm so happy for you! I couldn't help getting excited for him. He was an artist—a photographer to be precise—and he was quite gifted. Finally! After a few months of being depressed, this was a very good opportunity for him. It was a competitive field out there and that show was going to be his big break!

Opening my message from Blake, I suddenly felt warm knowing my friends were supporting me even if they weren't physically here.

From: Blake Knightly
Subject: Poppet
Hanging in there, poppet? Make it short and quick. No need to linger with the bloody tosser! We still have a few episodes to catch up with Game of Thrones so you better bring your cute butt back

home immediately! Or better yet—want me to come get you, Sienna? I'll book the next flight out or I could use one of the company jets to fetch your tenacious self. Don't doubt me because I bloody will drag you back to England, if I must. Two weeks without you or Toby (since he decided to permanently attach himself to Lucy's side) has been uneventful to say the least. The break-up with Camille didn't help much. The woman was painstakingly relentless wanting to move in with me. Got to dash, but don't forget about my offer about coming back early! I'm only a text or phone call away. I miss you.
 P.S. MAKE YOUR TRIP SHORT!
 BK

 Cute? My butt was anything other than cute! I got the junk to back it up. How could he say it was just cute? *Because he thinks you're just cute—you're just you, DUH?*
 I should've been used to it with Blake, I mean, we're friends, but as good-looking as he was, I wanted him to see the other side of me. Not the reliable, good friend side, but the attractive, sexy side of me, at least just once. But no, he has been impervious and treated me as nothing more than his buddy from his boarding school days.
 He and Camille broke-up? She wanted to move in with him after barely two months of dating? I could picture Blake's reaction perfectly; mortified, racing for the hills. He abhorred it when he felt as if he was being trapped. He'd confessed as much when I had first met him; he was in a similar predicament at that time, too.

Blake's message was just *so Blake*; it was bossy and demanding with a tad of adorableness on the side. If it were from any other guy, I'd think that he couldn't wait to have me back home and he was going ballistic from missing me. Sadly, though, it was from Blake. There was no hidden agenda there, plain and simple. I put my phone back in my clutch purse and swayed with the music, weaving my way to the dance floor.

One thing was for sure; you could always count me in for dancing. I loved to immerse myself in the music and just make my body speak as it moved to the beat. I danced when I was stressed out. I'd go to hip-hop classes or *Zumba* a few times a week in Hampstead. Chad managed the dance studio, and after closing time, we had our own little dance-off. It was our ritual and the bond that had brought us together.

Closing my eyes, I was swaying my hips slowly to match the rhythm of the music when I felt someone grab my hand. I opened them slowly, disappointed that it wasn't Kyle standing in front of me. I knew he was somewhere outside, possibly sucking face and swapping spit with his BB, but I couldn't help it. I was home and being home simply made me want Kyle, *badly. Maybe I'm nostalgic or maybe it's because I haven't been laid in what, like nine months? Who knows?*

"Hi! My name's James. Dance with me?" he asked smoothly.

Hmm, not bad looking. Quite decent actually. Not like Kyle, but decent enough and he seemed nice.

"Sure, James." I smiled at him as he twirled me around and my back landed on his chest. That was impressive. That man could dance. The DJ changed up the music to some Raggaeton song with Pitbull singing "Go Girl" and the tempo started to pick-up. Raggaeton music wasn't for sensual dancing. It was more for showing your skills with popping your hips and being sexy.

I separated myself from James and faced him. His eyes were all over my body and that gave me ammunition to get down and dance more. "So…"

"Sienna," I offered.

"Sienna. Where do you live? Somewhere close by?"

"I did, but I'm on vacation. Home is London, for now." I answered as my eyes scanned the crowd. The song ended and I found Jen across from me, watching us intently with our drinks in her hands.

Walking up to her, she gushed out, "Goodness, Sienna Richards! You know everyone was checking you out, right? You looked… *so, so* hot dancing out there! I was even getting hot and bothered watching you two dance and that's saying something! *Was that to show someone that you still got your groove on? Hmmm?*" I laughed. *Oh Jen! How right you are.* I shook my head in denial and smiled innocently.

"And who might you be?" she asked James who had unknowingly followed me. Cute.

"I'm James." At about five-ten and well-muscled with dirty blonde hair that was spiked, he was the epitome of boyish good looks.

"Where are you from?" Jen quipped. Knowing how she worked, she'd have him thoroughly grilled about his life in five minutes. We had always been protective of each other, so we tended to do that with most men we met.

Enthusiastically, I freed her hand of the Lemon Drop and took the tequila shot she was holding out to me as she commenced drilling. My, that burns. I welcomed the warm feeling it gave my body as I murmured "Thanks." She didn't seem to hear me, though, because she was still busy talking to James.

I, on the other hand, was busy scanning the room to see a familiar face. Okay, I was guilty. I wanted to see more of Kyle and what he was up to, but he was nowhere to be seen. I just couldn't believe he was being cold and indifferent towards me. What was that whole introduction scene with Brook, anyway? If he'd wanted me to think that he had moved on and was happier, then he'd definitely succeeded in getting his message across.

I decided right then and there that I wouldn't think about him anymore. Maybe this whole trip for getting closure from Kyle was merely stupid and irreparable. I couldn't torture myself with the thoughts of him with his girlfriend, kissing and groping each other somewhere in a dark corner outside. All I had to do was endure the night and move on, but for the mean time, I had to hold my head high, even if I was anguished with my heart gutted and intestines twisted inside out. Or I could possibly take Blake's offer. I could drown my sorrows happily simply by staring at him. Was this jealousy I felt? Or was it merely an indication that I was still *in* love with Kyle?

I love him. I've loved him all my life, but *in love* with him? I wasn't so sure anymore. I mean, *if* I was dangerously in love with him, then I wouldn't have left him behind to go to England, *surely?* I would have found a way to still be next to him or simply endured being miserable in Los Angeles if it meant being with him. I missed him and I was mad that he'd ended our friendship like that. I wanted to salvage our friendship, if nothing else. Before I'd left home, I had made that whole spiel of loving him, but I felt that I needed freedom. I desperately sought change, away from my horridly miserable past with my extended family and the memory of my dad.

Would I want him back if he begged me? *I don't know.* My mind couldn't process the possibility of us getting back together when it was blatantly apparent that he was in a happy, satisfying relationship.

Kyle took it badly when he learned of my plan. Of course, he was crazy about me. We were inseparable then. We'd even finished each other's sentences. We were happy together, but my soul needed something more, to feel free. Free from memories of my past.

So, my announcement to go to school in England was a surprise to everybody—most of all to Kyle. He didn't speak to me for days. He felt betrayed and implied I was giving up on us, our relationship. Distraught and wounded, he stuck it out until I left for school, showing me how much he loved me. Those few weeks before my departure were bittersweet. I remembered having a hard time letting him go at the airport, clutching and hugging him so fiercely. The memories brought a melancholy sigh and my attention back to reality.

"Well it was great to meet you, James," Jen said politely. I was still reeling from my nostalgic flood of flashbacks, swamped with the thoughts of what might've been. My mind shuffled back to the past and had lost track that I was here, in the middle of a damn party.

"Doll, can I speak to you for a sec?" Jen grabbed my hand and dragged me to a corner.

"Sure, be back in a sec, James." I gave him one of my melt-your-bones smiles for effect. It seemed to work from the look he gave me.

I needed a diversion and the unfortunate victim was James. I needed to gather my bearings before I went ballistic with roaring jealousy and did something drastic to get Kyle's attention, like going up to him and giving him a kiss that was extraordinarily scorching to the point that it would haunt him forever. So, I needed James tonight, for my sanity's sake.

"Hey! What's up?" I questioned her with an arched brow, knowing full well what she wanted to speak to me about.

"I'm going to leave the party with Ethan. He's off and another person is taking the shift, so we decided to go grab something to eat somewhere. Will you be okay if I leave and you catch a ride with Mickey or something? If you can't catch a ride, call me and I'll come get you."

"I take it Ethan's the hot-tender, right? Jen, seriously, go have fun. Don't worry about me. I have *only* two weeks to party and then back to school again, so I'll be okay. Go enjoy yourself! I'll see you tomorrow for catch-up and fro-yo, kay?" I hugged her and kissed her blushing cheek. It really bothered her leaving me here, but she wasn't my sitter. As much as I loved hanging out with Jen, she needed to enjoy and meet people. I wanted her to be happy, especially after Tony. "Have fun, doll." I gave her a huge grin.

"Will do! All right, catch up with you tom'! And be safe, 'kay? Call me if you need me, *anytime*."

"See you!" I shooed her away and went back to James who had been watching my interaction with Jen with hawk-like intensity.

"Did anybody tell you how gorgeous and sexy you are?" His dark eyes traveled all over me like I was a piece of candy to be savored.

"Are you just saying anything to get laid tonight? Because let me tell you, your line was way off the finishing line!" I instantly quipped back. *Ha! This is a merry-go-round play date buddy—nothing more,* I thought.

The last time I had sex, or any *intimacy* for that matter, was with Kyle. It was not that I didn't find anyone attractive in London—apart from crushing on Blake, but that was beside the point. He was nothing more than a friend. I had gone to a lot of house parties and met quite a few interesting and attractive men, but not one who'd given me the I-can't-breathe-and-think-around-you feeling. Maybe if I'd put myself out there instead of cutting them off before they could even speak it would make a vast difference. I should probably take up Lucy's offer of blind dates, just to dip my toes into the dating world.

Snapping back to reality, I gulped down the rest of my drink and placed it on the table next to me. The alcohol I had consumed was a potent mixture of vodka and tequila. A lethal combination, but it was the prerequisite of a person who was dealing with an emotional upheaval.

"Come on, James. Dance with me," I said invitingly. The music blared, making my feet itch to move on the dance floor and let loose, my body speaking through the art of dancing.

We were setting our rhythm as I danced against him, my back touching his chest. I let out a sigh. *Where was Kyle?* I thought sadly. *Stupid girl! Just let it go already*, I scolded myself. The dance was getting intense and James was gripping both of my hips, grinding and swaying slowly. I honestly didn't care because I wanted to forget, even if for only a few minutes. Then I'd go look for Mickey and ask him for a ride back to Jen's apartment.

James was getting *quite* comfortable. So comfortable in fact that he was moving his hands up and down the sides of my stomach. "You're so hot. I want you," he whispered in my ear. I rolled my eyes and ignored him. *Right, not going there buddy.* I was just using him temporarily for dancing, nothing more.

Am I a tease? Yes, definitely. *Do I feel guilty about it?* No, not really.

I closed my eyes again, feeling the beat and the alcohol seeping its way through my body. I felt relaxed and smiled, rocking the smashing beat with James. He was actually a descent dancer.

I felt his lips kiss my exposed shoulder, softly working towards my neck. His hot breath gave me a shudder. "James, I don't think that's a good idea."

Out of nowhere, someone yanked my right arm and dragged me away so quickly that my head spun. I barely got a chance to catch my breath. Everything was a blur— from the dance floor, passing the living room and up the stairs. Stumbling halfway up, I yelped from the tight hold on my arm. I tried to detach his fingers, but he was too strong. His fingers sunk deeper in my flesh, gripping it harder.

Sudden fear washed over my entire body. It was too dark, no light coming from the hallway or bedroom doors. *How am I supposed to take charge and free myself if I can't see my attacker?* I freaked and told myself to calm down and breathe. *Breathe. Think rationally, you can do this, Sienna.*

I was trying to get a handle on the situation and where the person was taking me. It was so dark, but it seemed like my abductor knew where he was going. The floorboards made a squeaking sound and the person holding my arm quickly turned around. Whooshing air swept by and there was an overpowering smell. A smell I *knew* so well that it made my throat constrict with familiarity.

Kyle. *What the fuck?!*

Five

"Excuse me! Where the hell do you think you're taking me! How dare you, Kyle!" Unleashed fury roared off me.

How dare he manhandle me like that!

He opened a door and brashly shoved me inside with him. I quickly scanned the room. It was dark, but it was illuminated with the glowing light of the moon from the bay window. The room was quite large, but uninhabited, a guest room perhaps.

I slowly glanced back and found Kyle looking down at me, furious to a point which I had never seen him before. My heart slammed wildly against my chest.

"Are you trying to embarrass yourself, *Sienna!*" he raged at me, face thunderous with seething anger. "Are you *trying* to prove something?" He glared and spit fire. "Are you trying to prove that you're a big girl, now? Taking offers and sampling men to your *liking*?" Kyle was accusing and livid.

"Excuse me? I was dancing with James! Mind your own fucking business and go back to your *amazing* girlfriend!" I screamed like a banshee at him. "And if I am taking offers and sampling them, it's my *goddamned* business. Now, leave me the FUCK alone!" I yelled with barely suppressed rage. *How dare he? After how he had* been cold towards me all night, without even a backward glance, and now he gives me this blasted brutish treatment? *Seriously*? I was done dealing with that crap; I was going home, back to London.

I tried to grab the handle of the door, but he quickly caught my hand and swiftly placed me on the wall next to the door. Both of his hands landed securely on either side of my head so I was imprisoned and had no chance in hell of escaping. I stared at him, wide-eyed and reeling.

Not only was I shocked at his attitude and his chauvinistic demeanor, but I was more surprised that he had even bothered to. "*Are you fucking drunk, Kyle?*" I asked him angrily. "Did you not hear what I just said?" He simply kept staring at me like he wasn't even listening to my questions.

He moved closer, his eyes burning into me.

I could smell him, his smell that I used to adore so much. The smell that reminded me of long nights sleeping in the nook of his neck. Being that close to him tested me to the hilt and drove me insane with acute lust. I was becoming nostalgic with pure longing.

His molten eyes roved all over my body, reacquainting himself with it. They stopped on my lips and his eyes darkened. My heartbeat quickened, my breathing shallowed. My body quivered from his close scrutiny. Goose bumps covered my body as my nipples tightened and my stomach had butterflies flying about. *Damn him.*

His gaze was too powerful and like prey, I was hypnotized and captivated by him; by his closeness, by that sudden reminder that he was my first love, my first everything. I closed my eyes and tried my damnedest to steady the wild beating of my heart.

His thumb traced my full, bottom lip slowly like he was trying to ingrain it in his memory. The moment his thumb grazed my skin, I was enthralled.

"*Sienna,*" he said my name in a whisper that was full of pain and hunger. My heart twisted.

I slowly opened my eyes and was tormented by the look in his. He wanted me. His desire was emanating from him; from every pore in his body. I knew that look so well. I suddenly had the urge to touch his chest, to feel his heat—his warmth—but I willed myself against it.

I wet my lips slowly with uncertainty and swallowed. I was having a hard time breathing. All I could hear was my heart pounding incredibly loud against my ribcage as I anticipated Kyle's touch. He would touch. That *look* said it all. He would devour me with no concession.

I stared at this man before me, wide-eyed and waiting, waiting for him to make a move... *Can I let this happen?* There was hardly any option of backing out. He was here for a reason, a man on a mission who would give no room for negotiation. *Oh, hell! I'm going to be in big trouble.*

He lowered his head to kiss me, softly at first, like he was trying to gauge my reaction, see if I would respond. I certainly did. I kissed him back, matching his pace as I was fighting all sorts of sensations inside of me.

A tidal wave of emotion rolled off me; from missing him to the angst of seeing him with a new girlfriend, amongst other things. All bottled in together once as I kissed him. My lips demanded just as fervently as his, like we couldn't get enough of each other. The titillating hunger was demanding his full attention, driving us both in a magical, wanton spell.

His signature smell enveloped me and I surrendered to the madness of lust and want.

He groaned as my fingers touched his hair and slowly traced his back, all the way down to his ass, cupping it hard with greedy hands and pushing him hard against me. The friction was palpable. We both groaned at once. *Yes, I definitely want this.*

How I've missed this man.

I opened both of my legs wider to accommodate him better, riding my miniscule skirt up higher, flashing my magenta lace thong. I couldn't stop holding him firmly and tightly by his ass, pushing him hastily and fervently against me to be nestled on my hot core. We both groaned in unison.

His soft kisses trailed down my neck slowly; he licked and nipped it. Writhing and panting against his hot body, I lost myself in the overwhelming, all-consuming need to be possessed.

His hand skillfully loosened my top, kissing his way to my very aroused and very erect nipples. He found one and playfully bit it. I whimpered from the pure ecstasy that was taking me to a whole different sphere of being. I was already horny, but that drove me over the edge of the precipice and straight into a state of absolutely wanton desire.

My thong was soaked as I rubbed myself with a driven mission over his jeans that showed his bulging erection. *God, he feels wonderful. Fuck.*

"Can I take you baby?" he asked in a raspy, sexy voice, panting with the need to consume me. It was full of promise, full of wicked urgency.

Of course, *that* was the old Kyle, my Kyle. "*Yes—yes.*" I was already out of breath. "Please hurry, I—" He didn't even let me finish before I heard him groan as he touched my thighs slowly, finding his way to the edge of my thong.

Thank god I had just had a Brazilian wax a couple of days ago, I thought to myself.

He slid my thong to the side and I felt him playing with my folds, gently torturing me as he teased them by making chaste, rhythmic circles around my sensitized mound.

"Take me!" I commanded. I couldn't focus on anything other than the throbbing, suppressed ache inside of me.

"Did you miss me, Sienna?" he whispered hoarsely in my ear. His hot breath sent tingles all the way down to my very wet opening.

I opened my eyes and looked him straight in his. "*Yes.*" I halted as he stuck a finger inside me, twirling and twisting it, hooking it in the upper wall of my slick channel. He frantically moved his fingers against my clit, flicking it up and down in a fast rhythm.

"Oh, my God" I yelped. *Yes!* I chanted in my head.

I grabbed his bulging cock and started to rub it hard before taking charge of his pants, swiftly opening the button and pulling his zipper down. His pants were pooling around his knees and I tugged his boxer briefs south, on top of his pants. I eyed him, *man he's aroused.* I gently cupped his balls with my left hand, squeezing them as I delightfully moved my right-hand up and down his cock, twirling his erection with voracious determination.

I was in such a delicious state of sexual euphoria, and I couldn't seem to hold it back, for much longer. Nine months of celibacy made me desperate for him.

"Kyle, please... *FUCK ME*," I pleaded.

"Not yet, baby"

Our foreheads joined together as we panted hard. His thick, rock-hard cock had a small drop of juice that was enticingly sitting on the head of his enormous manhood. I hastily licked my dry lips as I greedily eyed it. It was just waiting for my attention.

If he thought torturing me would work, then I would give him the same satisfaction. I slightly bent over again and licked that sweet juice off *oh-so-slowly* and at the same time, watched his face through my lashes with a pure fervor born of lust. Hovering over his cock, I sucked the head with just enough pressure to get all of his sweet, moist essence out, tasting more of his manhood as though it was nirvana. His face almost combusted with desire and he was beyond turned on. He seriously looked like a savage animal ready to pounce.

He took his fingers out and spread me against the wall. He kneeled down just above my throbbing pussy and hooked one of my legs over his shoulder as he opened my other leg wider. Licking my outer lips with his hot-teasing tongue while nipping and sucking, I buckled and threw my head back from the sensations racking through my body.

He quickly grabbed my hips and hooked my legs around his body as he pulled me down to the large bed. My dark mane of hair splayed everywhere. My top and skirt sat on my stomach, open and ready to be ravished. My thong was still lopsided from his drastic invasion and I was still wearing my cowboy boots

He loomed over me; his eyes intensely flickering to my nipples and wide opened legs. He pulled on his dick and started to stroke it, hard; big hands squeezing and stroking as I watched in fascination.

He took my boots off and pulled down my thong. "You're beautiful, Sienna." Our eyes locked as he gently rubbed me with his pulsating head, ready to combust. He teased and probed—driving me insane. I whimpered as I anticipated the feel of him inside me.

He paused, his cock just a mere centimeter from my soaked entrance. "Has there been anyone else? I know I was your first, but that could've changed since we broke up, so was there anyone else?" His face was passive as he waited for me to reply.

I shook my head. "No, no one."

His smile was predatory and victorious, eyes gleaming. He slowly entered me and pulled out almost immediately. "Baby, you feel like a virgin! *I love it that your pussy's like this. Best fucking pussy I've ever had.*"

I looked at him as he was watching our bodies joining together. He was staring down candidly as his cock slid cautiously into my tightened core. He seemed to cherish the idea of being the only man I had ever had sex with. He groaned like a caveman as he shoved his dick inside me, thrusting hard with no inhibition or restraint. My vagina's walls immediately enveloped him, accommodating his size.

"You're mine! All *mine!*" he growled like an animal. "I love how you feel... so silky, wet, and fucking *tight*. I've been constantly thinking about when I can have you over and over. I can't get you out of my head. When I saw you tonight, I couldn't help myself... I *needed* to have a taste of whatever you could give me. I needed to be *inside* you or I was going to go insane." He sounded raw with want as he picked up the pace and held my hips tighter. My legs were wrapped around his hips in an angle where it hit the spot, taking him deeper inside me.

Thrusting harder, filling me, stretching me, taking as much as he could with no restraint. His penis was undeniably stretching me to its capacity. I couldn't deny him that. I couldn't deny us both. Sex with Kyle had always been this good when we were together. So, it was hardly a surprise that we couldn't help ourselves.

I felt my body and pussy tighten around him, building up slowly for an orgasm. The friction was more intense, fervent and exquisite. I was almost at the tipping point and then I felt my body convulse around him as my climax came to a close. I held his shoulders, digging my fingers in and screaming hard as I came.

Kyle held my hips harder and placed his lips on my neck as he fucked me hard with building intensity, his orgasm trailing close behind my own. He screamed my name against my lips, "*Sienna, I love you. It's always been you.*" He then spilled his seed inside me with one hard thrust of his hips.

Thank God I had continued taking the pill.

Six

We held each other, panting and disoriented. I closed my eyes, trying to figure out what had just happened and how I could walk away from the situation without having my pride and heart trampled over. *Deep breaths. He said he loved me. He still loves me.*

I had so many questions I needed to ask him, but I couldn't seem to find the strength or the wherewithal to look him in the eye. I might've deluded myself that this was over... Could it be possible that it was one of those you-don't-realize-what-you-have-until-you've-lost-it types of things? I groaned. *I really am in the shitter.*

I slowly opened my eyes and drank him in. His hair and clothes were all disheveled and his eyes seemed to be raging something from deep within. He got up and started to get dressed without even giving me a glance.

Thinking about the fact that whatever comeuppance this situation brought, I had played a major part in it so I should hold my head high and act like the mature person that I am.

I sighed.

"Kyle," I whispered.

He was staring at the window, his back towards me like he was trying to gather his thoughts. Distant and unreachable. *Why isn't he talking?*

I straightened up my clothes and tried my best to fix my hair with my shaky fingers. I was nervous and anxious. I didn't ask for this, yet I couldn't stop or deny myself the opportunity to have him again. Even if it was for the last time.

Wanting him and for him to want me, it was just all too much and yet it was something I couldn't just walk away from. *Oh, damn it to hell and back.*

"Kyle, say something!" I croaked. Still no response. *What in God's name was he playing at?* "Oh! I get it! You just needed to get one last fuck out of your system and now you can just walk away! That's it, isn't it?" The feeling of being used was something I had never encountered before and that feeling didn't sit well with me, especially when the person in question was Kyle.

He moved against the window and the moonlight shadowed behind him, making him appear like he was some sort of dark angel, breathtaking to look at. This fallen angel was staring back at me with a blank expression. It gave me an idea of what was to come and for the first time, I was at a loss for words.

Seven

Kyle

God, she's gorgeous! Even in her bedraggled state from our crazy romping, she still had the ability to take my breath away by just standing there, demanding my attention.

Her skirt was twisted to the other side and not properly fixed. Her lips were red and swollen from our lovemaking, her hair disheveled and those beautiful crystal green/gold eyes flashed at me, immobilizing me on the spot from her sheer beauty.

She didn't have any clue how she affected me by just one look. She had that power over me. She had that effect on most men, but she didn't see it. I knew, though, and saw how men wanted to possess her; her beauty, her body, her beautiful heart. She was next to perfection. *She was also mine.*

How did I even manage to convince myself that I could be at the same party with her and not feel this? Savagely, I cursed my stupidity. She had always possessed power over me. No one had the capacity to drive me up the wall like Sienna could. When she was still here, she was *it* for me and yet she still walked away. I wasn't enough for her; never would be.

Chasing Beautiful 55

I have to harden my resolve for my sanity's sake. *God, this is difficult!* My throat ran dry as thoughts ran through scenes from a few minutes ago, vividly. How she looked lying there, waiting with desire—*all for me*. All mine and mine alone. Not any longer. She would eventually find someone; it wouldn't be hard. I bet there's already a line waiting.

The idea of another man possessing her brought ferocious feelings out of me. It was jealousy eating me alive. I couldn't go there. Not tonight.

"Sienna, I'm not going to apologize for this. Seeing you again made it impossible to resist you. I remembered us being good together and I just couldn't seem to help myself... I had to have you—"

"So that was merely a one-time thing then?" she cut me off in a shaky voice.

Her beautiful eyes were rimmed with unshed tears. How I wanted to possess that woman. My heart ached. I hated seeing her hurt, but I couldn't let her get to me. I barely survived when she left the last time. I couldn't go there again.

Steeling my resolve, I answered, "Yes, it is... it was. I'm with Brooke—" She didn't even let me finish before she started yelling.

"That's fucking convenient! You had sex with me without a second thought to your girlfriend and now, after you've gotten what you wanted, you're in a relationship again!" her voice screeched. Sienna was beside herself.

Man, she looked even hotter when she was furious. I wanted to take her again, right against the wall. *I'm going crazy*, I knew I was, but I truly wanted to reach out and kiss those pouty, swollen lips of hers senseless, for the last time. Just a little taste of her once more before walking away. *I hate feeling like this. This uncontrollable passion I have with her. I feel powerless against it. I have to get out of here—fast—before I start kissing her and fucking up more. Leave, now!*

I had to calm myself before responding to her accusing tone. "I didn't use you. I asked you if it was okay before things got way too heated and you told me it was fine," I countered. I wanted to be friends with her, but it was impossible for me. That's asking too much of myself, however I didn't want any hard feelings, either. "Hey, we'll talk this over when we're sober and calmed down. I'll come see you in a couple of days. How about we—" She held her hands up in exasperation.

"You know what?! This was a stupid mistake! I thought for a second there that... that you might feel something... or it meant that you still... you know what? It doesn't matter what I think! Let's forget this ever happened, 'kay? Please, don't try to contact me because I don't want to see or hear from you *ever* again!" she said with finality before she walked out the door.

Out of my life.

Again.

Hell, Sienna!!!

Eight

Sienna

London, present

"Sorry about that. I didn't leave you too long, did I?" A concerned look was etched on his face as he waited for me to respond to his question.

"No, it's fine. Stop worrying, Blake." I smiled at him. "Did anyone ever tell you that you're a worrywart sometimes?"

Sipping his coffee as he gazed at me, Blake waited a beat before speaking. "Yes, *you've* often told me."

"It's true. You've got to channel stress into something productive like *boxing*, perhaps?" I teased him.

"Sure, as long as you join me because then we can kick ass together," he jested back. Uh, not a good idea! I might just get turned on watching him; sweaty and full of angst.

"No thanks, I let out my frustration through dancing." I gave him a smug look. "Anyhow, what the hell happened between you and Camille?" I asked, using my casual tone. I was curious. I was always curious when it came to his girlfriends. Sometimes he was forthcoming with *the dirt* and sometimes he was tight-lipped.

Twirling his coffee cup, he studied it with the utmost concentration before he spoke. "As I said before, she wanted to move in with me. She was getting demanding, jealous and paranoid. It was nothing permanent and she knew it, still she pushed. So, I had no choice except to let her go."

"I really believed you guys were going to last longer than two months. I mean, you looked perfect together. Are you okay, though? I *know* for a fact that break-ups are nasty and never easy." I continued on when I didn't get a reply, "So, she was jealous, huh? Were you entertaining and catering to your other girlfriends, Blake?" I gave him a you're-such-a naughty-boy look because he surely was.

His throaty laugh filled the air. "Oh, Sienna, sometimes you're just too adorable. To answer your question, no, I wasn't getting my groove on and screwing other women. Honestly, she was jealous of my relationship with you. She thought we spent a lot of time together and that I was crazy about you. I assured her that we were friends, nothing more, and the mere fact that you were with Kyle didn't convince her troubled mind. Cam was convinced that once Kyle was out of the equation that I would step in and have you all to myself." Leaning back and still playing with his coffee cup, his eyes were steady and pensive while studying my reaction.

I laughed—*hard*—and almost ran out of air. *That's the funniest story I've heard,* I thought. Was Camille high on drugs? Had she looked in the mirror lately? She was *stunning*. Where did she cook up ideas like that? Blake didn't go for women like me. If he'd wanted to, he had plenty of chances over the last eight months, but he'd never tried anything that would imply that he was interested at all. So, she was being silly over nothing.

"Finding my story funny, Sienna?" He was still watching me intently, his voice steady and calm. He could be so intense sometimes that it made my heart skitter.

"Yes, I mean, come on! That was stupid of her! Why would she be jealous of me? Look at her and look at me. She's like the epitome of perfection. Besides, the idea of us? We'll never work. I mean, we like the same things, but we're different. You're like mega rich and soon you'll be running the world with just a bat of your eyelashes and I'll be, *you know*, the same. *Normal.*" My voice got small in the end. I bit my bottom lip until all the blood drained. The idea of Blake—*us*—bothered me. We were worlds apart. Everyone could see that. *So why do I wish that weren't true?*

He was still and unmoving, his lips in a straight line, pensive. *What's he thinking now?*

However he didn't have the chance to make a reply to my tirade because our food arrived and we fell silent as we worked on our plates, lost in thought. The food was excellent and I was happy to oblige my grumbling stomach.

"Mmm, this is definitely divine," I said as I bit into a piece of bacon, savoring every taste as I closed my eyes.

"Certainly looks like it," Blake murmured, locking his eyes on me as he took a bite of his toast.

Shrugging, I set aside my dish after I'd devoured every bite with pure gusto. I worked on my coffee next; I needed something to do besides looking at his magnetizing eyes. Uncomfortable was not the word I would use to describe it. Breathless would possibly be fitting, though.

After what seemed like five minutes, he threw down a hundred pounds on the table and asked, "Ready?"

"Not really, but guess I have to see what's in store now, don't I?" I stood up and pretended to be petulant.

"You'll just have to wait and see, my impatient one."

~S~

"Notting Hill?"

"Yes, our next stop to your easing-up-the-pain strategy." Blake smirked when he said *easing*. Ha. I would rather forget that embarrassing incident in the car right before breakfast.

He parked the car, got out and opened the car door for me. I smiled. "Hummingbird Bakery?" I gleefully asked.

"As you wish, milady," he said with a little bow. That gesture put me in mild hysterics. He had a good sense of humor. That was why we were friends. We could act silly and have fun; it was easy.

Grabbing my hand and pulling me next to him, we strolled along, passing clothing boutiques and antique places. Notting Hill was a gem. They had a lot of funky, trendy stores and just about any knick-knack you could ever imagine. It was awesome!

We made our way to Hummingbird Bakery that made these delicious, mouth-watering cupcakes. Each perfect bite was sheer bliss. Still holding hands, he guided me inside the shop. We had found the bakery simply by walking around on a Sunday afternoon and we'd both fell in love with it; each liking to indulge our sweet tooth. So, once in a while, we would come here to indulge. Though, on special occasions—like when it was that time of the month for me—he brought me a box of cupcakes to cheer me up. *How thoughtful was that?*

Ogling those beautifully decorated, earth-shattering pieces of ambrosia with yearning eyes, my mouth salivated. Blake ordered red-velvet and chocolate chip cupcakes to be eaten outside on the patio as well as a dozen more to take home. Oh, yum! *You see how intuitive he is?* Ha!

"Let me pay for this one," I demanded. He gave me a shut-the-hell-up look.

I huffed and turned around as he paid for the cupcakes. It was always like that with Blake and Toby. They would get offended if you offered to pay. Some men would gladly appreciate the offer. Some men expected women to pay half of everything, but those two still believed that they had to take care of the ladies. They felt insulted if I asked.

I found a table for two and waited for my cupcakes to arrive. Sitting, I basked in the warmth of the sunshine hitting my face. *Life isn't so bad when you have cupcakes*, I mused.

"Here we are!" he announced as he placed two of my favorite cupcakes in front of me and cut the cupcakes in quarters. We had a ritual because we both loved these flavors, we agreed to a compromise, eating them half and half. It was kind of cute.

He took a piece of red-velvet and fed me. I opened my mouth, closed my eyes and savored the flavor. I was a passionate person, especially when it came to food.

"Mmm, yes!" I purred in satisfaction.

He laughed. "I knew you wouldn't be mad for long." He gave me his god-like smile again, placing his ray-bans atop his wavy hair. I looked away. He looked too tempting and when he smiled like that, I had this urge to stare and worship him. It was very disconcerting to feel that way sometimes and it caught me off guard.

He was a great friend and a flirt, but a great friend nonetheless. So, when he acted a certain way—holding my hand and smiling at me like I was the only person in the world that mattered—it confused the shit out of me.

My phone beeped so I took it out of my purse and checked the message.

Kyle.

Heart-thudding, I opened the message.

Nine

From: Kyle Matthews
Subject: Miss you
   I went over to Jen's to check if u were there last night and found out u went back to London. Why? Did u leave 'coz of me? Wanted to speak to you. WE HAVE TO TALK about what happened. About us. Call me. Seeing u again made me realize how much u mean to me, Sienna.
   I'll be waiting for your call.
   I miss u,
   Kyle

Shit. *How do I reply to that?* He sounded guilty as hell. Well, he should be after he treated me crassly with no thought to my feelings. He just took what he wanted and my feelings, *again*, were pushed aside.

"Sienna, what is it?" I turned off the screen, slid my phone back into my purse and sighed heavily. "Kyle... he wants to talk."

"Are you going to?" He looked at me, pensive, unreadable.

"No, I'm not giving that jerk the satisfaction," I said with decisiveness and a clear voice. I had made up my mind. As much as it killed me to admit, I was *still* hurting.

What hurt more was the fact that he dated her a month before breaking it off with me. He didn't even have the decency to end things before saddling himself up to someone else. To put icing on the cake, he had sex with me and *still* went back to her. Now he had decided that he wanted to *talk*? The nerve!

"What's up next?" I asked, studying his unreadable expression. He grabbed my hand and played with the inside of my palm with his middle finger; in slow, agonizing, fever-inducing, rhythmic circles.

He was touching me *a lot* today. He never used to, I mean, apart from the usual greeting of kisses, hugs and nudges here and there; nothing as personal as this, though. I was afraid to ask him about it, so I pretended it didn't bother me, as if we did this all the time.

"It's a surprise, poppet. I'm sure you will figure it out soon enough." Getting up and hooking my left arm around his, we strolled back to where his car was parked.

Walking at a leisurely pace, my thoughts raced back to Kyle. Was it cold of me not to bother replying to his email? We had been through a lot and I considered him family. My mom died giving birth to me and my dad died when I was seven. From what I could recall of my dad, he was a loving man, giving, and he adored me. He used to talk about Mom all the time and how they had loved me from the moment they discovered she was pregnant.

Dad had a heart attack. No one saw it coming; it was abrupt and swift. All of a sudden, I was alone. I remember the conservator consoling and assuring me that my father was a wise man, that he had invested the insurance he got from my mother's death shrewdly. He even added that there was more coming from my dad's insurance policy, amongst other investments he delved in. My dad made sure I had a college fund on top of everything else.

He basically thought it out accordingly, just in case he died. I received a partial amount of his Social Security money to tide me over until I turned eighteen; the legal age when I took over my own spending and could handle all my finances. At the time, though, I could have cared less about money because all I wanted was my dad back.

My father's sister, Christy, took me in. She had a husband, Dan, and a daughter a year older than me, Caroline. It was hell living in the Brown's household. I was the interloper who basically ruined their neat, consistent lives.

When I met Kyle—the boy next door—he became my solace, my protector and my friend. His mother was always kind and loving to me, baking cakes and pastries that I enjoyed through the years. I had grown to depend on Kyle, and leaving Los Angeles had torn me apart; but I had to leave home. I needed to get away; to have a new life, a second chance to erase all the memories of what I'd endured living with the Browns. As a result, he was hurt, but supportive about my decision; or so I'd thought.

My father had indeed made sure that I was well provided for. The money I had gotten from him on my eighteenth birthday was substantial. I don't need to work if I don't want to, but I have other plans. I want to become successful on my own and thrive in the marketing industry.

~S~

Leaning back against the cool leather seat, I exhaled. *Boy, I'm exhausted.* Driving around town seriously took a toll on my jet-lagged condition. I closed my eyes and tried to clear my head, the sounds of Moonlight Sonata in cello relaxing me into slumber as he squeezed my thigh.

"Don't drift off yet. I promise you can sleep when we get to our destination, all right?" Blake glanced at me with a hint of a smile. He took ahold of my hand and placed it on his lap; overwhelming me with weird emotions.

I turned sideways to look at him. With his shades on, he looked like a sexy man from a car commercial, only a tad bit more good looking. He resembles Gaspard Ulliel or Christiano Ronaldo; that's how deadly he looked. The Latin coloring and charm contributed from his Italian mother combined with *when he spoke Italian...* total, major turn on. His eyes were another dynamic aspect that contributed to that killer look. Blake had the most unusual eyes; midnight blue, rimmed in silver with flecks of scattered gold in the middle. When he was angry, his eyes turned almost black; making those scattered gold flecks stand out. It was like staring at the Milky Way galaxy as it s*ucked you in* until you were lost in them. It was spellbinding and disconcerting at the same time.

"Are you done checking me out, Sienna?" He gave me a sideways glance before diverting his eyes back to the traffic ahead. *Busted.*

"Not yet, just give me a few more minutes; I'm sure by then I will have memorized all your flaws," I quipped back. I was a tad mortified that he'd caught me staring wide-eyed at him. "Are we almost there?" I drastically needed to change the subject back to safer ground.

"Yes, a few minutes or so then you can sleep, my sweet; just as long as you promise not to snore." He smiled tenderly at my horrified expression.

"Ha! I do not snore!" I pinched his leg.

"Ow," Blake yelped, but had his god-like smile in check—dreamy was the more appropriate term for that smile. I hated it that he had a way of disarming me with that smile.

As promised, after a few minutes we arrived at our destination; an upscale hotel in Knightsbridge. Getting out of the sexy Aston Martin, he handed the car keys to the valet attendant and tended to me. With a hand on my back, he gently guided me to the hotel spa.

"Aw, how you read my mind, Knightly! Thank you! Thank you!"

"I hope this will make up for all the energy you invested with me since this morning. Come." *Like I wouldn't forgive him?* Blake held the door and we stepped inside the reception area which was a white and glass combination, giving a chic, clean-cut effect.

"Mr. Knightly, welcome back!" greeted the auburn haired, blue-eyed, svelte lady with a flirty smile.

"Krista, hello! How are you?" Blake said, acting polite yet distant.

"I'm very good, Mr. Blake." Krista gazed back through her lashes, quite suggestively. With a few taps on her keyboard, she spoke again, "Okay, your room is ready. Olga will show you to it." I caught her wink at him and bite her bottom lip.

I almost grunted out loud from her obnoxious, flirty attitude. *Disgusting much? Jesus.*

Olga appeared almost immediately and politely showed us to our reserved room and I couldn't have run out of there fast enough.

My massage haven awaited.

Ten

The moment I walked in, I felt like I had walked onto a set of the *Arabian Nights*. The room had an oval-shaped pool that was decorated with rose petals. Further to the left stood a colorful silk tent with beaded throw pillows and kaftan rugs. Plus, there were large, glass bowl-stands with petals and floating candles embellishing the room.

The masseuse tables, situated at the edge of the tent, sat about ten feet from a lightly-lit fireplace. The strategically placed scented candles made the ambiance intimate, seductive and downright romantic. The room *smelled* of romance, a mixture of roses and berries with hinted notes of vanilla.

I was guided to the 'his and hers' changing rooms, where it was requested that I wear this skimpy, barely there thong. I smirked. *Great, how the heck will I ever be comfortable lying next to Blake almost naked?* If I could relax, I was going to doze off the minute those powerful hands started kneading my back; I was sure of it.

Is romance what Blake has in mind? Is it possible? Why would he book a suite? He could've gotten separate rooms, but he didn't. *So, if it is, am I ready to date him?* I was and I wasn't. I had just gotten out of being with Kyle and I was sure as hell was not emotionally ready for someone as intense as Blake. That was like taking on Hurricane Katrina. Besides, he didn't seem to be keen on long-term relationships anyway.

Apart from Kyle, I hadn't been with anyone else; emotionally or physically. Blake was a very intense person, too. How the heck would I handle him? I had watched as women became beyond helpless when he ended it with them. They were hysterical; calling incessantly, hoping he would take them back. He never did. It was mayhem.

No, thank you. I didn't want to be one of *those* women. *Risking our friendship over sexual satisfaction? Maybe?* I shoved that thought quickly to the back of my mind.

I came out of the changing room dressed in a thong and a robe. I made my way towards the massage tables where my masseuse, a tall, stern-looking man—possibly Eastern European—waited patiently for me. He introduced himself as Alec.

Blake was already on his stomach and had a scant towel draping his glorious ass. His back was all ripping-hard muscles, defined and cut. He had his head down, even though the session hadn't started yet. I was sure he'd done that to make me feel less uncomfortable when I tried to position myself on the narrow table.

Hopefully, that scant towel will be enough to cover my bottom. Alas, as dreadfully predicted, it just *barely* covered it. Most times, I was proud of my "well-rounded assets," but at times like these, I wish they were a little less rounded.

As they started working on our backs, Blake turned, reached out and touched my arm softly. "Feeling better?"

I smiled shyly at him. "Yes, thank you. It's exactly what I needed. Next time, I'll be the one giving you surprises, though." His beautiful face lit up, giving me a devilish grin.

"I'll hold you to that!" I nodded, tranquility washing over me as I closed my eyes while I continued facing him.

Shouldn't I be mourning the loss of my relationship with Kyle? Yet, from the moment I opened my eyes today, Blake had railroaded my thoughts, putting Kyle somewhere faraway and distant. Except for the email...

How was *that* possible? I was crying my eyes out last night and, today, I felt like an entirely different person.

Powerful hands started to work their way down to my lower back. Hovering around where the slope of my butt started. Kneading thumbs and fingers made the towel slide lower. I gasped from a jolt of pain and then exhaled deeply, lips slightly parted. The pain felt good and I welcomed it. The stress I had from the last couple of weeks had taken its toll on my body.

Opening my eyes, I found Blake staring intently at me. He didn't smile or speak; instead he kept those magnetic eyes locked onto mine. I swallowed, nervous. Those eyes had the power to penetrate and reach inside of me. It was disconcerting. *He's been doing that a lot today.*

Not knowing what to do, I closed my eyes again. *Christ, I'm so screwed*! Heaven help me if he did try something.

God knows I had a hard time resisting Blake when he asked something of me, however this Blake—pure full-on Casanova-mode Blake—would be my undoing.

The smell of roses and the crackle of fire lulled me to sleep, unperturbed and tranquil. I happily dozed off into a blissful slumber.

I woke up from the soft click of a door closing. Befuddled from my nap, I glanced around and realized that I was alone, lying there, almost naked and asleep.

The darkened lighting from the candles made it hard to see much further into the room.

"Blake?" I called out, sitting up and looking for my robe, but it seemed to have vanished! It was nowhere in sight.

Biting my lip, I pulled my long hair forward to cover my breasts; it was good enough to cover my nipples, but not enough to cover the outline of my boobs. I tried to gather my wits.

"In here!" called out Blake. Where was *in here*?

Slowly, walking barefoot in a thong with my boobs partially covered by my long hair, I glanced around in the dimly lit room. "Blake!" my voice laced with urgency. I started to make my way to the pool area, but couldn't see him.

Instantly, out of nowhere, he started gliding from the darkened corner of the left-side of the pool.

My eyes rounded in admiration. My, God! I'm going to have a heart-attack.

Gaping at his muscled pecs, six-pack abs and his wet hair swept back; I felt a jolt of instantaneous lust. I swallowed hard. He was absolutely breathtaking. *Wow. I've never seen his chest before. NOW, I really think he was made perfectly!*

Rooted to where I was standing, heart beating erratically and *barely* breathing, I was mesmerized by his sheer beauty. I barely forgot to take note that I was almost as naked as he was.

"Care to join?" he asked, glancing at me with the same look he'd had at the massage tables. He looked like he was ready to pounce. Still and waiting... The look was full of yearning... and pure, blatant lust.

My stomach flip-flopped.

Standing there—virtually naked—I was staggered, astonished.

Being in that room, with *him*, the air—the smell of heady perfumed roses, the darkened setting of candles, making the room glow—I suddenly felt like I was there purposely to do his bidding!

Enraptured and enthralled, I slowly walked to the pool, joining my god-like mortal of a man without breaking eye contact.

I went into the pool that was scattered with rose petals. The water gently rippled as I went deeper in, but I stopped when the water barely hit the tips of my hair.

Standing on the very last step of the pool, I looked over to where he stood, unmoving like a statue, although his electric midnight eyes, roved all over my body, branding me. I gasped from the burning, ardent-filled scrutiny of his roaming eyes.

He moved towards me, his tanned, rippling body glistening with water. My eyes examined his abs, slowly making my way to his hardened chest, his broad shoulders, his neck, his enticing lips, until my eyes stopped at his burning, silver-rimmed, midnight blue eyes.

The air was charged, electric and perfervid.

Looking up to his face, I was stunned frozen. He was so tall and all-male.

I gasped again as he traced his thumb over my bottom lip, his eyes darkening.

"You look like a goddess; exquisite and beautiful," he rasped out as the back of his finger gently stroked my neck and collarbone with utter concentration. I shuddered from his delicate touch. "You don't know how long I've been waiting for you, my sweet Sienna. I've always wanted you—from the moment our eyes met. *I wanted you, badly*, but you were with someone else. I've been patient—biding time—until you were free, and so here we are."

I drew breath and slightly wetted my dry lips. *He'd always wanted me? What?! This was insane! How the heck did I not see this?*

Being with Blake would be passionate; thrilling and tumultuous, however, did I have the capacity to go through a circus ring? I wanted him, no doubt. My mind boggled; I couldn't think straight. As much as I was attracted to Blake, I didn't know if I was ready, *just yet*. He was too intense, too commanding, too everything. At the same time, I was hypnotized and my mind was beyond puzzled. It really was disconcerting.

"Blake, I—" I looked at him with beseeching eyes, licking my dry lips. "I don't think I'm ready for this. I mean, I'm attracted to you, but this is too sudden. You must see—understand—that I *need* time." I searched his eyes as he studied mine, waiting for him to answer me.

After what felt like forever, I saw him nod his head. "All right, my lovely Sienna. I've waited for eight months; I can wait a little more. I'll wait until you are ready, but I want to make something clear, I don't just want you for your body... when you're mine, I want your all; *your body, your soul, your mind.* I will consume you. I'll be your world and in return, I'll worship the ground you walk on and make you a very happy woman," he spoke with a strong, decisive and determined voice without his eyes leaving mine.

He wants me. Blake Knightly. Wants. Me. I was excited, yet at the same time, I wanted to run for the hills.

"Blake, if you must insist, but until I make up my mind, you have to respect my boundaries." I gave him a peck on the left cheek, moved a little closer to his ear and whispered, "Thank you." I accidentally grazed my nipples on his chest and the friction tingled all the way to my core. He immediately hissed through his clenched teeth. *Oh, my God.* That felt wonderful.

"Sienna, try not to test my limits because I would gladly throw caution out and take you right here until I've had my fill of that glorious body; until you're limp and worn-out from me fucking you," he warned me with tested patience.

"Right"

What the hell do I say to that?

I stepped out of the pool, leaving him as his powerful gaze burned holes through my back. I daren't look back unless I wanted to play with fire. He was searing, scorching and sizzling with fire waiting to be unleashed. *ON. ME.*

Shit.

Eleven

I woke up startled from my surroundings and it dawned on me that I was in Blake's apartment. The bedroom was simple with a touch of understated, warm elegance and twice the size of my room. A modern, queen-sized bed sat in the middle of the room with russet-colored, damask patterned wallpaper. The other two walls were painted an ecru shade, complementing the chic design. Amber colored lamps made of an actual rock sat on both sides of the bed. A contemporary chaise lounge in pistachio silk slanted in the corner along with a large antique mahogany coffee table. The room basked aglow with three shaded, floor-to-ceiling glass windows, overlooking the streets of Mayfair.

His entire apartment, which was the whole tenth floor, was styled in the same manner; modern contemporary and expensive French antique accents. The combination gave the whole place subtle warmth. I smiled. The comparison of the apartment and its owner was uncanny.

I gently rubbed my eyes as I yawned. Events from yesterday flashed through my drowsy head. He drove us straight back to his place from the spa. Surprised, yes, but I was too exhausted to argue with him to take me back to my own place in Covent Garden. Deep down, I was pleased that he'd wanted me to be close to him.

He cooked dinner and it was superb; I hadn't known he was such a skilled cook. After we ate, we caught a couple of episodes of *Game of Thrones* from the DVR player. We lounged with a bottle of red wine and chocolate truffles from the famous La Maison du Chocolat—a completely marvelous way to end our day.

During the entire evening, he never once tried to make a pass. He was respectful and kept his distance, though he did find ways to subtly touch me. *Whereas you turn into a brainless creature every time he does touch you?* I was aware of him; whether he was in the room or not.

He acted like the usual Blake and that put me at ease. I was relieved. My mind was confused when it came to him. I mean, I know what *I* want, but when he was being all sexy and seductive, my thoughts turned to mush and that was perplexing.

When it had been time for bed, he'd handed me one of his silk boxers and a shirt to wear. He decided—without asking me—that I should stay with him for the next few days until Sunday, when Luce arrived.

School started Monday as he, too, began his lengthy training to become a tycoon like his grandfather. Blake would be shadowing him until he was ready to retire, which loomed on the horizon. Blake had been learning the ins and outs of the business for the last two years, but this time, he'd take on most of the responsibilities. His grandfather wanted Blake to take over as soon as he'd deemed him ready.

Their family business was vast from what Toby had told me. From oil to five-star restaurants, real estate, hotels and casinos, merely to name a few. I doubt their family would be estimated to be worth billions without an enormously diverse portfolio.

Blake knew full well that his granddad would not be there forever. He needed to prepare for the inevitable, hence the prepping and training of him at the age of twenty-four. He's almost four years older than me.

The only thing that I was worried about was Blake changing. He was rich now, making a lot of money from his own investments, but when the time came, when he could tap unlimited funds and resources while being surrounded by powerful men as well as the world's most beautiful women, I was afraid that would change him. I heard Toby joke about it before. I was quite certain that he too believed it was possible. Money and power could be intoxicating, especially at Blake's impressionable age.

I stretched for five minutes or so before going to bed. It helped me sleep better and my body didn't ache as much if I stuck to one side during my entire sleep. The moment my head hit the pillow, I immediately went to sleep. Sometime during the night, I felt him bend over and softly brush my cheek with his lips and whisper, "Sleep well, my Sienna." Then he quietly left my room to go to his own.

I slept like a baby after that.

Still lounging in bed, his beige, fifteen-hundred count Egyptian cotton sheets haphazardly tangled on my legs, I looked across the room and stared at the sky through the windows. I felt well rested and *almost* like I was myself again.

My face heated and my stomach coiled as memories of the pool incident surfaced. I groaned. *Damn that man. He looked so good. That body... my God.* Thinking about it made me all hot and bothered. I would never, for the life of me, fathom how I managed to decline his offer last night. It would undoubtedly baffle my psyche for the rest of my life.

Not hearing the door creak open, I was surprised when Blake sat on the bed across from me, amused and sexy as hell. "Devising a plan to stay in bed all day, poppet?"

If he only knew... how long can I endure this longing for him before I succumbed to what my body is aching for?

I noticed that he had light stubble growing on the sides of his face; it made him utterly and painstakingly gorgeous. *How does one manage to look beautiful after waking up in the morning? I bet I look a fright.* He was wearing a fitted, black shirt and sheer, black cotton pajamas; I would not have guessed in a million years that he was a pajama man. I would have thought commando was more along the lines of his thing.

I looked away from his face. He'd caught me studying him several times already—much to my growing embarrassment—I didn't need him catching me yet again.

"Can we please? I need to just rest and unwind," I exclaimed. I was still tired from my trip.

Watching me intently, he reached out, brushed the hair off my face and tucked it behind my ear.

"As you wish."

I looked up, smiling and meeting his gaze. "*Really?*" I asked, loving his easy, jovial demeanor.

"Yes, *really*!"

My laugh abruptly halted as he slid his body next to mine. I stiffened when his strong hands pulled and hugged me from behind. The sudden feel of his hard, chiseled chest made me shudder. I was frozen in shock. *Body, what happened to waiting?*

I want you... my damn mind kept nagging.

His strong hand snaked around my waist, holding me tightly, imprisoning me to the feel of him. The heavy thud of his wildly beating heart was proof that he was as affected as I was. My body was shaking with hunger for Blake; a hunger that seemed to be getting close to impossible to *resist*.

"Hmmm... I just want to *smell* you. I hardly slept knowing that you were sleeping in the next room. Can you grant me this small request, my sweet Sienna?" My body shivered with anticipated excitement. I nodded, urging him on.

His lips touched softly behind my earlobe as he trailed soft kisses all the way down to the base of my neck where he neatly pulled my hair to one side, exposing my neck and inhaling deeply. He groaned with frustration and a burst of lust surged from my aching core.

Just one kiss, I thought wildly. *I just want a taste.* Turning around to face him, we stared at each other intently. An electric current between us crackled and sizzled. It was heady, intoxicating, searing.

My gaze fell on his lips. *One taste, that's it.* Feeling bold, I licked my own bottom lip. *It's now or never. Do it.* Slanting my head, I kissed him very softly. A guttural sound came from his throat as he devoured my lips. His kiss was demanding with potent alacrity as I matched his passion.

This. Gorgeous. Man. Wants. Me.

Hooking my leg on his hips, I locked them against me. The feel of him being *this* close drove my body to a raging inferno. *I'm so screwed.*

Feeling brazen, I tugged and pulled his shirt off. I needed to *touch, feel, taste* his hardened chest. I greedily stroked his chest as his kisses became rapacious. Encouraged from his groans, I kissed his neck and ran my whole hand on his chest, scratching his erect nipple.

"Ah," Blake hissed from pain and pleasure.

He speedily flipped me on my back and kissed my swollen lips hard. He briskly opened my boxer-clad legs and positioned his hot, hard body above me. Our tongues clashed as I locked both of my legs around him; his erection pressed boldly against his sheer pajamas. The heat of his erection rubbed with urgency against my covered mound, sending me into a tailspin.

We were on fire. I felt his need, his frustration, his want and desire from his blazing kisses. The mixture was heady and downright intoxicating.

I broke away from his mouth and moaned satisfyingly. The profound effect his body had on me was astounding. I felt drunk and more aroused than ever before.

"Blake," I gasped with my sex-awakened voice.

Gazing at me with lust-filled eyes, he ground his hips harder onto my core—making me even wetter. *Touch me. Please.* Panting hard like he'd run a marathon, he sat back, looking over my wanton state. *I can't breathe.* Time stood still. He softly caressed the cleft of the boxers, over my mound with his finger.

I whimpered and bit my lip, *hard. Blake... what you do to me...*

The evidence of my arousal seeped through the soaked silk fabric, wet and hot. His finger grazed it, teasingly and stopped right there while he held my gaze, and then spoke. "You're so beautiful. You have *no idea* how much I want to fuck you, hard and fast as you scream my name when you orgasm. I want to feel you come apart while my cock fucks you harder." Oh, shit. My throat ran dry, his eyes pure with torment. "You have no idea... how much this is killing me, but I'm keeping my promise. *You will be mine, Sienna.* Not just for your body, I want *everything* from you. I'll wait. You're worth the wait." His voice was gruff, but very much determined.

He shrugged and looked away. *Was he for real? What if I just want to get laid without the emotional hang-ups?* "Blake—I—are you serious?" I croaked out, wide-eyed in disbelief.

The infuriating man kissed me softly and then quickly pulled his body away. "Breakfast will be ready and waiting in ten minutes." With that, he left the bed and exited the door with an evident hard-on.

I was left with my mouth agape and still wide-open legs, waiting to be ambushed. *Who. Does. That? How can he just walk away when I'm more than willing? Because it isn't only the body he wants to possess. He wants me— body and soul—and he won't settle just for my body. He wants it all.*

He wouldn't change his mind, either. He wouldn't make another move until I'd cleared my emotional closet and cleaned up all the cobwebs hanging loosely about. *How long will that take?* I cursed. *Blake. Fucking. Knightly.*

Twelve

Showered and dressed in Blake's Manchester United football jersey, I piled my hair up and went straight to the kitchen. Upon entering, I stood frozen and watched as Blake placed an omelet and some bacon on each plate. His hair was still wet from the shower and he was barechested, wearing only his well-worn jeans while also barefoot. His defined torso and six-pack made a rippling effect as he moved about. My mouth watered. *What is it with men in jeans and bare feet? The combination's simply irresistible!* Was he trying to drive me insane? *He looks so deliciously yummy!*

Feeling my presence, he turned around. With a sexy grin, he sauntered to where I was standing, kissed my forehead and guided me to sit at the breakfast bar.

"Coffee?" the hot chef asked. I nodded, unable to speak, still mesmerized by the charming, barefoot-jean-clad god. He went over to the coffeepot. My eyes gawked as his impressive back muscles flexed when he moved. I restrained from licking that nicely sculpted back and that nicely dipped curve along his spine. Yum!

This man is too sexy; it's criminal.

I could stare at him all day without becoming bored. It was like eye porn and he was a delectable subject. At the same time, though, I wanted to throttle him. Here he was, acting like a good host, as if he hadn't left me hanging and yearning in the bedroom.

Coffee poured, he fixed it to my liking and placed the steaming cup in front of me with a sexy smirk. Blake's eyes twinkled. He was enjoying this. His eyes were dancing with amusement. Asshat!

"Blake, can you please put a shirt on?" I demanded petulantly. I didn't think my hormones could take another dose of this exuberant display of masculine perfection.

He just gave me a devilish smile and teasingly said, "Is it too much for you, Sienna? You just say the word and we can remedy that problem, *immediately*."

I shrugged. *What word? How about three words? Let's just fuck?*

"Thought you needed a reminder—that we'd be *explosive* together." That hoarse, gruff voice again. It was making my body hum like no other. "But I want your all, poppet."

Don't I know it!

"Baby steps, Blake." There was no doubt in my mind that we would be explosive, but I was trying to delay the inevitable. Once I let him in, there was no going back. There was no doubt in my mind that he would take everything; he would consume me without concession.

It would be easy to fall for Blake. Most women did, but I would be vulnerable, open, defenseless.

~S~

"Loser!" I proclaimed with a little victory dance, hands waving high and hips swaying.

"Don't count your eggs *yet*, two more games to go," Blake declared playfully.

We were playing Scrabble. *I'll show him who's the BOSS!* I had won two-to-one and he was a little annoyed because I kept teasing him. This was the second time I'd won a round with him and we'd played possibly a hundred games all together. I was ecstatic in my victory!

I was dancing one of my victory dances again when he pulled me to the couch and tickled me until I was out of breath, panting loudly as my thoughts were provoked. I badly wanted him to kiss me again, but he never tried. I wouldn't beg, though I was dying inside. It was as if the incident this morning had never happened. *How does he switch off like that? Hot and smoldering one second to casual and friendly the next?*

~S~

Standing in the open, built-in wine cellar, I was biting and twisting my lips in frustration. My indecisiveness was causing me to contemplate for the umpteenth time as to what kind of red wine to drink when he snaked his arm over my shoulder and grabbed his preferred wine.

"Do you feel like a bottle of Barolo?" Blake asked close to my ear. His question barely registered because I was hyperventilating.

I cleared my throat before I responded with a steady sounding voice, "I was actually thinking of Pinot Noir or *that*, but you've made up my mind. Go get the wine ready. I'll go fetch the popcorn, Parisian cake and the fruits."

I could get used to this domesticated scene with Blake. He was so easy to be around; charming, thoughtful, witty and *sexy*, but most of all, he made me laugh. It wouldn't be difficult to fall in love with him.

We watched another movie, our third one today. *Love Actually*, one of our favorite movies. It was funny, sad and heart-warming at the same time. I snuggled close, drawing his heat and the need to be near him. He pulled me closer and placed my head against his strong, solid chest and held me firmly. I listened to his heart beating steadily, closing my eyes as he started to stroke my arm gently and I sighed with blissful contentment.

Life certainly was starting again, whether I wanted it to or not.

Thirteen

The sound of my ring tone blaring jolted me awake. I was about to reach for my phone when it suddenly dawned on me that there was a strong, heavy arm clutching my waist.

Blake.

I turned around to see if the noise had awoken him, but his steady breathing showed he was fast asleep. I unhooked his draping arm carefully as I slid off the bed, grabbed my phone from the side table and left the bedroom as I softly made my way to the living room.

Why did Blake sleep next to me? He didn't the night before last.

Either way, I was happy he did.

The entire flat was dark, but the moonlight helped me find my way around. When my toe touched the plush, black area rug, I opened my phone to see who the caller was. *Who would call me at this time of night? Luce? Jen?*

Kyle. It was him. Again.

I might as well get this out of the way. If I have to start considering being with Blake, it was best to clear out as much "Kyle baggage" as I could. The other issues I had would continue needing to be worked on. I'd have to talk to Chad, my gay, go-to person and a very dear friend, about this. He's my unofficial therapist.

After a couple of rings, he picked up. "God, Sienna! I've been going crazy here! *Are you okay, baby?*" Kyle sounded frantic and like he *was* going crazy. *Why is he still pursuing this issue? He made it perfectly obvious what his intentions were the last time I saw him.*

"Yeah, Kyle; I'm great! This call better be important if you had to wake me up at *FOUR* in the morning. So, what do you want, Matthews?" I sounded exactly how I felt; furious and annoyed.

"Jesus, baby, take it easy, will you? I've been trying to reach you, but you've been ignori—"

"It was done with good reason, Kyle! I told you—very clearly in fact—not to contact me again. But *no, no, no!* You never listen to me. I'm hurting; that's a given. It wasn't just our dating relationship that ended; I lost my childhood best friend, too! *So, am I okay with that?* Not really, but it was *your* choice. It was *your* choice to go behind my back—*cheat*—and start dating Brooke before having the decency—*like other men do*—to simply break-up with their girlfriend first!" I shrieked with erupting anger.

I heard him sigh, heavy and pained. "I'm sorry, Sienna, *baby*. I've been missing you so badly. I've been drinking non-stop and got a DUI. I had a hard time handling things without you. *I am hurting, too.* You left me, even if it was for school... but you left and went on with your life without me. When you called, happy and excited about your day, *I felt left out.* It had been you and me against the world since we were kids, but in the end... there was *just me.* I was lonely—I needed you—but I couldn't beg you to give up your life for me. You already went through so much with your family. I can't ask it of you. Breaking it off was the best thing to do, —and I was getting by... trying to live my life... working harder on my career. It was helping and, for the first time since we said our goodbyes at the airport, I felt like I was living again." He drew air into his lungs before continuing. *Crap.*

"When you showed up at Katie's party, everything went down the drain... all the things I told myself that had helped me get through were forgotten the moment I saw you again. You looked even more beautiful..." He sounded choked up; his thoughts and feelings unconcealed. My stomach churned.

"I simply wanted you—*I needed you, I still need you, Sienna*—like air to breathe. You're my life and I can't just go on living and not be with you. Without you, I'm in hell. *I'm desperate for you...* and without a doubt... in my mind—my heart—I'm *still hopelessly in love* with you, Sienna," his voice was barely a whisper. I wouldn't have heard him if the apartment wasn't so eerily quiet.

Oh Kyle! This conversation's killing me inside. He was dying from pain. I felt it. I felt his pain and it tore me up inside because I didn't want him to hurt. *I love him, but I can't go through this; I'm beyond hurt.* The man who I'd placed so highly on a pedestal had crushingly betrayed me and appallingly let me down. That was something I couldn't get past or forget about.

I sighed with a heavy heart, the weight pulling me down, "Kyle..."

"Sienna..." His voice came out gruff and anguished. "Please, please, I beg you. All these years I never asked much from you, but I'm begging you now, give me another chance. Let's give us another shot. I won't let you down this time. I promise you I'll figure it out, speak to

Dad and work in our branch in London. I'll do anything. *I'll promise you anything.* Just please, think about it? We can get married, if you want... I'd give anything to have you back... just please, Sienna, forgive me and love me again."

He sounded so broken and extremely desperate.

I sat on the floor, leaning on the couch with my lips quivering. What he said broke me in two. If he had come clean and been honest about his feelings, we wouldn't have broken up. We would still be together. Plan our lives, get married and have babies. It was what we talked about. He had thrown that out the window because he was lonely. I had been lonely, too, for the whole time we were apart, but I hadn't acted on it. What I wanted most was trust, honesty and loyalty and Kyle lost on all three counts.

Can I take him back? After what he's done, I could, possibly, try to see if things could work out if he'd showed remorse and guilt. I might've before—before Blake told me how he felt about me. Hold on, did he say anything about what he felt? Besides wanting me? No. He hadn't. His intentions were clear, though. He wanted me, in his bed, yet other than that, he'd never spoken about any indication about the future. It was sex he was after—my whole cooperation—but not once did he mention he was after my heart.

I mentally shook my head. *It doesn't matter.* My heart was not up for anyone to grab. Love made you weak and opened you up for pain and suffering. Never again! I took a chance with Kyle because he had been everything to me, but he'd reinstated my beliefs by proving them right.

"Kyle, I forgive you. I do. It would have been easier for us if you'd told me about your feelings then—how terrible it was for you—but you never uttered a word to me about your pain and I'm sorry for that. I am. However, asking me to give us another try? That's a bit too much. I can't trust you. You hurt me and I'm not ready to forgive that yet. I'm so sorry for everything, but it's all too late now; I can't be with you," my voice trembled because each word punctured me deeply.

Never in a million years had I imagined that I would cause Kyle pain and suffering. I wanted him to be happy and part of me continued to want to take all that pain away. He meant that much to me, but I couldn't sacrifice myself for his happiness.

I just couldn't.

"So, please, I'm begging you now, Kyle, I need space. I can't talk for a while. Maybe in a year we could be friends again, who knows? However right now, I simply can't. We just have to move on with our lives, separately. Goodbye, Kyle... I'll always miss you." Those last two sentences were torturous to utter. The pain in my heart was so acute, I gasped for breath.

I immediately ended the call before he had the chance to speak. I almost ran to the bathroom across the hall, but I was careful not to make a lot of noise and wake up Blake. Blake awake was the last thing I needed right now. He'd grill me until he'd gotten all the facts as to why I was distraught.

The bathroom was dark and comforting. The moment I closed the door, I slid down it and sank onto the cold marble tiles then cried, *hard*. I cried because Kyle was the only family I had growing up. Because he was my best friend, my first love.

It hurt, but I didn't have it in me to forget what Kyle had done. He made his bed. He simply needed to grow up and accept that sometimes things just didn't work the way you pictured them.

After weeping for what seemed like an eternity, I washed my face and swollen eyes. I stared at the mirror, studying my distressed state, complete with blotchy skin from crying. *That's enough crying. You've shed it all and you have nothing left. Be strong.*

I walked slowly back to the bedroom and positioned my body next to a sleeping Blake, curling up, closing my eyes and praying for sleep to come so I didn't have to think about my life. Even if just for a little while. Experiencing this kind of loss certainly made me realize that life would never be the same again for me.

Kyle. He'd always be a part of me. I would always remember him as the man who took me in, held me close and protected me. He was my hero, my love, my best friend.

Goodbye, my Kyle. I will always miss you.

Fourteen

Waking up the next day was brutal. My body was lethargic and my head pounded. I groaned and covered my head with a pillow. As much as I wanted to stay in bed all day, though, I knew that I needed to keep moving to find some sanity.

Reaching for my phone, I was shocked to find that it was already eleven-thirty. *Haul your lazy butt out of bed, Sienna.*

Sitting on the bed, I decided to text Chad.

Me: *Hey, love! Are you busy? Want to meet me @ the studio to let off some steam? -S*

Dragging myself to the bathroom, I washed my face and brushed my teeth then studied my reflection. My eyes were red and swollen from crying, my skin blotchy and my hair was a tangled mess.

Oh, Kyle! What a disaster.

After I had showered, I changed into my freshly laundered dress that I'd worn a few days ago. It was time to go back and change. As much as I liked wearing Blake's clothes, I missed my own. Putting on some gloss, I went to go look for him and found him in his library which also served as his office. He was on a call in a heated discussion and engrossed with something on his laptop. I backed away and went to the kitchen to give him time to take care of whatever was so important.

I sat at the breakfast bar enjoying my coffee and croissant when I received a text from Chad.

Chad: *Sure, baby love. What time do you want to meet? I'm free now. Want to grab lunch somewhere? Or better yet, how about I come over with Chinese? xxx*

Smiling, I eagerly replied to meet me at my apartment in an hour and Chinese would suffice.

I put my phone down, sipping my coffee and enjoying a buttery croissant when Blake strolled in with what seemed to be an empty coffee mug and a serious face.

"Everything okay?" I inquired lightly. Wondering where he'd gotten his mood from.

Blake shrugged. "Just work. We're trying to open a hotel and casino in Marbella and there seems to be a problem with permits as well as budget overruns that I have to look into."

"That's unfortunate. I hope you guys can figure out a way to fix that. Marbella's a prime location. I'm sure you and your people will figure out a way. You're good at that."

I melted when he gave me his sexy smile. "Thanks for the vote of confidence, poppet."

"Anytime, Knightly" I winked at him as I retreated back to nursing my coffee.

"Going somewhere?"

"Yeah, I'm meeting Chad for lunch at my flat in an hour and we'll hit the studio later in the afternoon, perhaps."

Blake turned and walked over to the coffee pot. Stirring his contents with two teaspoons of sugar before returning to his former post, leaning against the kitchen sink. "Sounds like fun! Will you be back here tonight?"

"Do you want me to? I'm sure you're busy with work, Blake. I don't want to impose any longer."

He left the sink, came over to where I sat and swerved my chair so I sat there facing him. "Listen, you're not imposing. I invited you to stay here. I would love for you to stay with me tonight before Monday comes. We'll be busy, but always count on me to make time for you."

Swoon.

"I love spending time with you, too," I said shyly. I was still not used to being with Blake like *this*. It caught me by surprise every time.

"What time do you plan to leave? I'll take you," he said over his coffee as he took a sip.

"Are you sure? Aren't you busy with the Marbella project?" He couldn't keep pushing his work aside for me. I didn't want him to get into trouble with his grandfather.

"*Yes*, but I'm still taking you. End of Story."

Bossy aren't we?

"All right, in that case, save dinner for me. My turn to cook."

"Brilliant! Apart from your coffee making skills, I haven't tried anything else." Blake was back to teasing.

I punched him lightly on the arm. "Hey! Don't make fun of me! I'll load your dish with cayenne pepper just to punish you for that!" I happily grinned at him.

"*Oh, really*! My type of punishment will make you suffer with sweet torture. So watch it, my sweet. Take *only* what you can handle." Threats, though hot, but threats all the same.

Am I one to back down? Don't think so, buster!
"We'll see about that, Knightly," I retorted, amused.

He held my hand as we both got up and he went to fetch his keys to drive me back home to meet with Chad for lunch.

Fifteen

"Have some room for dessert, love?"

I looked at Chad, astonished that he could even stuff himself more, considering how much Chinese takeaway he had consumed. "Go help yourself; I'm in a coma." I moaned as I gently patted my belly.

"We'll just do double time with dancing tonight. It's okay; cheesecake?" Flagging a forkful of blueberry cheesecake in my mouth.

I groaned in frustration with his persistent attitude, knowing full well I had a weakness for sweets. Evil man! *Heavens! That was delicious.*

I got up and went to the kitchen to prepare some coffee. When I came back, Chad was already almost halfway done with the cheesecake.

"Is something's bothering you? What is it, baby love?" He glanced at me with a perfectly arched, ebony brow. This was as good a time as any.

Feeling helpless and confused, I spilled everything about Blake. They were friends by association, therefore Chad didn't know I had the hots for Blake Knightly and my confession shocked him.

He whistled after I finished with my tale, took a big gulp of coffee and looked me square in the eye, "Wow. That's some story." Chad lightly fanned himself. *You don't say, buster?* I smirked. "I'm usually pretty good at these things, but I never once thought he saw you that way, love. I mean, apart from a few lingering glances here and there... Wow, that man can certainly put a mask on! God, I can't believe you didn't just shag him! How could you not even think of going all the way, love? I would've yelled at the top of my lungs and told him to *'pummel me any way you want me, baby!'*" Chad looked all hot and bothered all of sudden. I was sure his thoughts involved the sweaty, smoldering hot body of Blake. I had no doubt in my mind Chad would do exactly that. We both had the *hots* for Blake Knightly.

I laughed loudly and then, smiling at my dear friend, I confided, "I was sort of ready to do it all the way, but he resisted and I admire him for that. It's difficult enough that I just barely got out of a relationship. Don't get me wrong, I *like* Blake—more than I should at the moment—and when he's around, he's all I think about, but I'm not emotionally ready. I'm drained and I can't simply put myself in that situation. Not right now, maybe in a few months. Blake's an intense person. He will consume me and I'm not ready for that kind of emotional rollercoaster. Not yet."

It was very confusing to be in this position. Here I was, trying to gather my bearings after such a riotous upheaval with Kyle and a whirlwind of hotness of the formidable god that was Blake Knightly had been added. What was a girl to do?

"Even though he's a deliciously sinful specimen, I get where you're coming from," Chad sympathized. "Maybe you can still have fun with him without getting too attached? Or you can just enjoy being single and see what's out there. God knows you haven't yet experienced London single! Maybe it's time you should, love! I'll be with you all the way! This is so exciting." He looked wistful, like he was imagining all sorts of scenarios in his head. *I bet his are more revealing than mine.*

Blinking a few times, I leaned back on the couch and exhaled, sighing. Chad had a point. For me to jump from one relationship to another was not good, *everyone knew that*. I still had baggage to sort through with Kyle. I couldn't think about him without feeling a heavy knot in my chest. Everything was unbelievably complicated.

"You're right. Maybe being single is the answer to all this."

"There you go. Speaking of fun, I have a different motive for coming here. I need a model for my theme with the art show I have in eleven weeks and I want you to pose for me... with a male model, who I don't know at the moment—"

"Pose?"

"Yes, pose! Model for me! For my grunge sensual theme—"

"I'm not model material, Chad!"

"I beg to differ. Have you seen your body, Sienna? C-cup breasts, small waist and that ass! Although, most of all, you are gorgeous! You look sensual and you fit my theme. I don't see anyone else that would be as fitting, baby love. Do this for me and I'll be forever in your debt. Will you do it, love?" He was on his knees with a huge pout and dark eyes, pleading. Chad, with his flair for the dramatics, didn't exactly hold back when he was desperate.

This meant I was the only person he had in mind. *Sigh, the things we do for the people we love.* "Ah! How you tug at my heart. You just have to go looking all sad! Fine! I'll do it! You can bet your skinny ass that you'll be indebted to me for a while! When does it start?"

"I have to speak to a few guys tomorrow. I'll let you know by Tuesday. Shooting will be in around a week or two. The images I want are risqué and you'll be technically nude with undies, just to warn you." He looked delirious and sheepish at the same time, happy that his project was well on its way.

Technically nude? Shit. Bite me. I pulled my legs to my chest. Thoughts of the shoot mocked my mind. What if it looked obscene and tacky? "These better be tasteful, Chad," I warned.

Chad merely huffed. "Baby love, I only do it *with* taste and class! You know that!" True, I did know that. His artworks were appealing and riveting. I was sure my lack of confidence came from my own insecurities.

After lunch, we left to go for a walk around Bond Street and went inside Selfridges before hitting the gym. He needed some apparel and he enjoyed modeling them as I sat, cheerfully critiquing his choices.

A couple of hours later, we left for Hampstead and hit the gym. They have floor-to-ceiling-mirrors that surround the room. There were six rooms in total and we took one that wasn't occupied.

Damp with perspiration, I gulped a whole bottle of water. The four sets of samba gave me a much needed workout and it felt great.

"Get your sweet, Brazilian ass back here! Time to shake it for Salsa!" Chad called out as he was jumping about and browsing through his iPod.

"Coming!" I yelled as I made my way to the middle of the room. I studied the image before me. Dressed in my black leggings and cut-off, loose shirt that hung off one shoulder, I looked flushed and glowing.

The two-hour workout with Chad had left me in a happy state as I made my way through the checkout counter in Waitrose on Marylebone High Street. I was going to make spinach salad with cherry tomatoes and stuffed mushrooms, lasagna with hot Italian sausage instead of beef, garlic bread and tiramisu to finish the meal.

I paid for my items and hurried outside to hail a cab. Sitting comfortably inside, I texted Blake that I was on my way with groceries in hand and to meet me in the lobby.

Sixteen

Playing with my wine glass, I took a sip and looked at the man across from me. His fitted black shirt emphasized his bulging biceps and broad shoulders, making my thoughts slide downwards into explicit territory. "Blake..."

He looked up from his tiramisu. "Hmm?"

"Is it okay if we keep this—*whatever this is*—between you and me? Until, I've thought things through?" Right, like *whatever this is* would be a suitable description.

Something passed in his eyes before he responded, "If that's what you wish, then, I'll oblige, Sienna."

"Thank you. Since we're on the subject, what is it you're really after? A relationship? A fling? *Friends with benefits?*" The list could go on really.

"A relationship, but as I said before, it's your decision. I am not going to pressure you to do anything you don't want to, however if you are, I want everything and *only* you, exclusively. I don't share what's mine." That was good to hear. I mean, I didn't want to share him if he was giving me the goods.

"I see. That's a lot to take in." I looked up to him with a serious expression because the damn atmosphere had dropped and it was becoming quite serious.

"It is. That's why I want you to think about it carefully." Blake leaned back on his chair, studying my reaction to his words. His eyes were cautious and gauging.

"What happens to our friendship? I don't want to ruin what we have. It's a major factor for me." It was one of my many fears. Blake and I could lose a lot if things turned ugly.

"I know and our friendship means a lot to me, too, but I want you! I'm *burning* for you, Sienna. I can't seem to get you out of my head! It's driving me insane. It's the only thing I can think about; *you're* the only thing that I think about. I can't think straight, Sienna!" Blake's face was unashamed from his admission. If anything, he looked unfaltering. He was a man that knew what he wanted.

I was starting to become weary. "How about we try friends with benefits? No strings attached kind of thing first?" *Say yes*, my thoughts pleaded to no avail as he shook his pretty head.

"No. I *want* all the strings; the good and the bad. If it's too much to be with me because you're still recovering from your ex then, as I said before, I'll wait. I want you to want this, too; badly enough that you can't wait to be with me. I want you open only for me and no one else." *My. He just keeps on pressing and pushing forward, doesn't he? Fuck, he's so damn delicious, too.*

His unabashed admission turned me on while it also gave my stomach butterflies. I desperately wanted to kiss him. Blake was the kind of man who knew what he wanted and didn't hesitate to get it; he could be utterly ruthless.

"Why me, Blake? I know you don't do serious relationships. I mean, you have so many women who don't have any emotional hang-ups or issues. I just don't get it; you could have any woman you want. What makes me different compared to Camilla or the others?"

"That's easy. You're different because you're all sassiness and sexiness; well, most of the time, however sometimes you can just be gullible. You're unique and I've never felt this connection with anyone. It's exhilarating and terrifying at the same time. I knew this even before we kissed, which merely confirmed what I knew. You feel it, too. I've seen you trying to tame it down, yet it only intensifies. This is the point of no return for us, Sienna. You know that."

Point of no return, he said. *Did I know that?* Yes, I sort of did. Blake didn't do things in small measures and I was next on his list, apparently.

"It's like that, huh?" I gave him a teasing smile as I got out of my chair and walked across the table to where he was sitting. His face lit-up with a knowing smile.

Does the bad boy want to come out and play? I thought provokingly as his smile became dangerous. Oh yeah. He definitely does!

I stopped before him, hooked my right leg to the other side of the chair and straddled him. He gasped at the sudden contact of my body. Without hesitation, I took his face with both of my hands and kissed him passionately, *deeply*. My kiss showed him how much his words affected me. How he made me forget about everything except for him.

The kiss was ferocious as our hunger battled against our tongues. I pushed my ass down harder and ground against him. We both groaned as his hands gripped my waist, pressing me firmly in place against his jeans that revealed his hardened shaft. The friction was pure torture. The heat of his rock-hard erection against my soaked underwear was madness.

My body took over; I suddenly felt possessed, wanting to feel more of him as I rocked myself slowly against him. I was on fire as I kissed his neck, sucking it until he moaned my name. I slowly kissed him as I became lost in this blanket of mindless lust with this beautiful man. The spiral feel of emotions rocketed through my body as we devoured each other. My heart ached. I wanted him. So. Badly.

However, what tore me up inside was the prospect of losing him altogether as my dear friend. He meant a lot to me and, by sleeping with him, there was a huge possibility that our friendship could not and would not survive.

Breaking from our locked lips, he touched his forehead against mine. "You've enslaved me, but I'm asking you to stop torturing me. *End my agony. Say yes.*" His voice sounded different; it was pleading and laced with hungered passion. It simply thrilled me to the core. I had this power over him, and for a man such as Blake, that was something important. I heeded.

"Blake—"

He took my chin and looked me straight in the eye. "Be mine, Sienna. Your body tells me that it's mine, but your mind resists. Stop fighting it and let it conquer us. We're fated to be together. I knew it from the moment I met you. You were made for me." *How sure could he be?*

"Blake, I can't have sex with you tonight... but I can help you. I'll help you... get off..." My voice trailed off, lust-filled and with purpose.

Empowered from his reaction, I made up a plan. I might not be ready to do the deed, but I was ready to have fun. *What fun it'll be, too.*

I peeled myself off him and lead him straight into the living room. I dimmed the lights and directed him to sit on the couch. "Take all your clothes off except your boxers." I commanded with absolute seriousness.

Walking over to his iPod player, I chose the song "I've Been Thinking" by Handsome Boy Modeling. It was fitting for what I had in mind for him. When I turned around, he was already situated in the middle of the couch and oh so ready! Blake's compelling eyes preyed on me, scrutinizing each move I made. His smooth, six-pack abs and torso looked too tempting not to be noticed. His black boxer briefs fit him like a glove. My, oh my, what a package!

I swallowed and started to panic. *Shit cakes. Do I know what I'm doing? You've got it under control. You're fine. You can do this! Now, move.*

"I need to get something. I'll be back in a flash and don't move an inch, Knightly." I almost *ran* to the bathroom, fetched what I needed and darted back to where Blake was patiently waiting for me. "So, where were we?" I murmured as I got close to him. "Oh yeah, pleasing you, Mister Knightly." Smiling and biting my lip, I felt excited and wicked at the same time. I felt like I was on top of the world when he looked at me.

Opening his legs a little wider, I stood before him with my long, dark hair wild and mussed-up, lips swollen from his kisses. I untied the knot at my neck and pulled my short dress above my head, slowly and deliberately, making a teeny show for him as I let my dress drop on the floor.

When I heard him groan, it was exactly the push I needed. My eyes took him and his reaction in. His face was stoic as his eyes darkened, making his gold flecks stand out, his gaze penetrating me, burning unadulterated fire. With shaky hands, I unhooked my bra, swiftly pulled it off and seductively placed it on my fingers, letting it dramatically drop to the floor. I stood before him with my hot-pink lacy thong and four-inch, patent nude, Rolando Louboutin pumps.

Still, no sound came from him, but his eyes spoke volumes. They were locked on my round and heavy breasts. His penetrating gaze alone had the power to make my nipples harden and my womanhood drench with excitement.

Strategically bending over him with my butt in the air, I kissed his neck and slowly made my way to his tanned and chiseled torso. I licked the outer part of his nipple until it hardened and covered with goose bumps. My hot tongue flicked it slowly and my teeth playfully bit it.

He gasped. "Fuck, Sienna. You're killing me." Slowly, but surely, they say...

Glancing at him through my lashes, I gave him a cat-like smile. "I've only just started. Be patient, young man!"

I went back to assaulting his left nipple then took my other hand and scratched the counterpart. Blake buckled. I smiled. *You like that, don't you?*

My tongue snaked slowly to his navel and I nipped around it. My fingers traced the outline of his boxer-briefs, soft and light, only enough to make him tingle. I wanted him hot, ready and rabid.

My fingers gently pulled down his boxers and I gasped loudly from his springing cock. It was massive; the girth was thick with a big vein that outlined his hardened ridge. *Wow, impressive!* My eyes were greedy, my mouth watered and my hands itched. *Hell to the mother fucking yes!*

I gathered my bearings and hastily pulled the boxers off his long legs. Kneeling, both of my hands gripped his thighs. I kissed his inner thigh, slowly and deliberately, as I made my way to his balls. My hand cupped them, *hard,* and started to play with them—massaging and pulling a bit. Holding his balls firmly, careful not to touch his ready to combust cock, I slowly got up and bent over to kiss his neck. My lips assaulted; sucking and biting his earlobe while my hand continued to grip and squeeze his balls.

"*Sienna,*" Blake muttered, edgy.

I felt his large hands cup and grip my ass. He gave my left butt cheek a loud spanking. "Ahh!" I yelped from pleasure, but he needed to hold back. It was my playtime, my show. "Naughty, naughty. Don't touch, Knightly." I hissed.

"I can't help it. Your beautifully shaped arse was right there just waiting to be spanked."

"Enough," I scolded the Brit.

He immediately shut his mouth when my hand found his manhood, stroking it slowly, up and down its silky, hard length. The gesture made him close his eyes with his mouth hanging ajar.

"You like that, Mr. Knightly?" I inquired with a raspy, sultry voice. I licked my lips as I watched my hand touch him, his shaft got bigger and bigger.

"*Yes,*" he responded, his voice thick and throaty.

Still stroking him, I used my other hand to reach for the oil and flipped it open. I drizzled and smothered it all over his throbbing cock as it freely oozed all the way to his balls. It wetted my hands as I massaged it on his body, spreading the oil all over his thighs, his torso and on my breasts. Once done, I retreated back to catering his hardened ridge.

Right-hand on his cock and my left on his balls, stroking his lengthy cock slowly as I sucked his balls and played with them with my tongue. He rasped my name as if in pain. Easing my mouth slowly from his sack, I gripped his hardened length and stroked it as I covered his engorged head with my other free hand, swiping my oiled fingers at the crown, making delightful friction on his manhood.

Blake instantly buckled from my assault. "Fuck!"

Encouraged, I gently squeezed the head of his shaft as I rotated my hand, upping his pleasure as I simultaneously stroked the rest of his cock all the way to the base with fervent concentration. Blake was moaning my name, uninhibited in his delirious state. I accelerated the speed once I felt him grip my shoulder and pant loudly.

Oh, he's so close. I want to see this compelling man come apart in my hand, in my mouth.

My determined tongue viciously caressed him as I touched my hand to his ready-to-combust head and massaged his balls. My hot, greedy mouth swallowed his swelling crown. I sucked him, hard. My tongue flicked on the small, slit opening of his shaft, where his creamy juices come out, before I hastily retreated to the bottom of his head where it was extremely sensitive, teasing him relentlessly.

I bobbed my head, twirling my tongue around his crown as my tongue swiped and stroked him harder, taking everything I could from him. Blake took my head and clutched his hands in my hair, firmly holding me in place. With another strong flick of my tongue, he finally surrendered, yelling my name as he unloaded himself in my mouth. I sucked him hard, devouring every drop of essence that he secreted out; leaving not a drop behind.

Blake gasped for air as he stared wildly at me, fascinated. I pulled my mouth off his cock; his cum still sat creamily on my tongue. Without blinking, I wantonly gazed at him through my lashes while I swallowed his creamy seed, *slowly,* and licked my lips after. Boy did that ever catch his attention.

Hell, Blake even tastes divine. Midnight silver eyes blazed, never leaving mine. Blake hastily pulled me down on the couch and swiftly placed my hot aroused body underneath him. His dominating swiftness left me ravenous. To say my body was humming would be an understatement. At this point, it was singing at the opera house.

When he managed to find my lips and sealed them with his, he kissed me with pure abandonment. I kissed him back, matching his passion.

I felt drunk with lust—with need—all because of Blake. He did things to my body that I couldn't explain. It kept exploding when he was near, like he was the puppeteer and I was merely his puppet.

My pussy throbbed and my thong was beyond soaked. I was more than ready. Blake broke off the kiss, sought my neck while his hand cupped my breast, squeezing a hard nipple as he fiercely bit my neck.

"Holy. Shit. Blake!!!!" I screeched.

Blake's still-hard cock teased and rubbed the outer layer of my barely covered mound "You're drenched, Sienna. Are you sure you don't want me to remedy that?" His roughened voice was hoarse against my ear and it made me shudder.

How I wanted him... to feel him inside of me, but it was not the right time.

Groaning my name loudly, Blake took his cock and determinedly guided the head around my pussy. Coaxing the lace with one swift nudge of his engorged head to move the elastic lace sideways, my swollen lips exposed to his assaulting eyes and awaiting cock.

Blake's eyes glittered.

Not, yet. I pleaded in my hazy mind, *not yet.*

"God, you're beautiful, Sienna." He softly rasped out as he gently parted my pussy with his cock. The engorged head gliding, slowly and gently, as it rubbed against my clit. *Dear me. That feels blindingly exquisite.* "I know we can't have sex. Don't worry," Blake gently assured me. I nodded, trusting him fully.

My chest heaved and my eyes closed. *Blake, what are you doing to me?* I felt like a whole different person, not the old Sienna, but someone wanton, shameless.

My thoughts departed as he teased the tip of his head around my opening. Circling it slowly, *excruciatingly,* until I was delirious from pleasure. His lips planted kisses all over my stomach and then he placed his mouth directly in front of my pussy. I hooked my leg on top of the couch and the other on his shoulder. *God, YES!!!*

"Open your eyes." I did as he commanded. "Never take your eyes off me. Watch what I can do to your body."

My eyes were the size of saucers, my mouth agape as I saw his tongue taste me with a slow flick, sucking my dripping clit. Blake took his thumb and played with it some more. The image of him going down on me, tasting me, was carnal and erotic. I almost lost it. I was mesmerized and couldn't take my eyes off him. My body was already strung out, but the raging onslaught of his tongue was too intense, and suddenly, I ran out of breath as my body quivered, responding beautifully to him.

"Come for me, my sweet Sienna." His mouth was unrelenting, savagely caressing my pussy as he inserted a finger inside my molten opening. The pleasure it gave me was unbearable. My orgasm was closing in on me, fast.

My breathing halted when I felt him insert another finger inside. It found my spot and he rubbed both his fingers there, ceaselessly. "Yes, give it to me. Please!" I begged as I gripped the couch, scraping it with my nails as my orgasm rocked me in waves. My body twitched from my release and I was panting, out of breath.

Whoa!

I closed my eyes and sank back on the couch. *Energy all spent*, I thought contently as I limply moved my hand to cover my eyes. *That was mind-blowing!* Never in my years with Kyle had I experienced anything like it and that was only his tongue and fingers. Imagine what his cock would do to me when the time came. That thought alone made me want to jump on him and find out. I did say Blake made me shameless, didn't I?

Spent, Blake placed himself on top of me. He kissed my lips gently and tenderly. "Now, we're even." *Hell yeah! What a payback it was, too!*

He kissed my nose as he slowly got up and then swiftly plucked me off the couch as if I weighed nothing. Blake headed towards the bedroom and placed me carefully on the bed before he slid in next to me.

"Wow. Just wow," I whispered in awe.

"I know. It makes me wonder what fucking you would be like," he wondered out loud as he kissed my earlobe and tugged me closer to him. "One day, you will be mine. All those sweet juices will be for my mouth and my cock. You won't want anyone else."

Hmm, smug, aren't we? "Arrogant man," I mumbled softly.

"No, just being truthful. You gave me something tonight. The memory of you almost naked, stroking and sucking me, will forever be ingrained in my memory." *I'm sure it will.* It was what I wanted to do.

I laughed sleepily.

He kissed my shoulder, hugged me tightly and whispered goodnight. His soft breathing hit my neck as we both fell asleep.

Seventeen

Monday came with a rush. My classes were a little hectic. From marketing classes to Art History, I was sure I was about to spend a lot of time studying paintings in The National Gallery to catch up.

I came home yesterday after spending three nights with Blake. Luce came back upbeat from her vacation with Toby and things seemed to be going pretty steady between the two. I was keeping my fingers crossed. I never once mentioned to her that I'd slept in Blake's flat or any occurrence I'd had with him. I wanted to keep it to myself for now.

Blake had been texting me about how his day was. He mentioned how hectic his schedule was going to be, but asked if I wanted to have dinner with him Friday night. I eagerly replied and said yes, of course. I liked how he was being patient with me. I was even surprised that he was willing. The Blake I knew didn't wait on women; it was the other way around. They waited on him. I hoped, though, that he wasn't risking our friendship because I was simply a novelty. I guess I just had to wait and see how he fared with the situation.

By Thursday, I was tired and weary. I hadn't been sleeping properly. My thoughts lingered at night and it had been driving me insane. I hadn't heard from Kyle either. I was relieved and saddened at the same time. *Will there ever come a time that I won't feel this deep anguish every single time I think of him?* I was haunted by that last phone call; his voice desperate and pained. I truly hoped that he was doing well and not indulging himself with alcohol until he was numb from the pain. I'd never known him to be so irresponsible. That's why it was a surprise that he'd gotten a DUI.

I was sure his parents were overjoyed with that news. I could seriously see their shocked faces and the disappointment. They were a lovely couple. They loved Kyle very much. Chris Matthews and I were friendly, but we'd never been close. Kyle's mom Marie, on the other hand, was a dear and had made me feel right at home ever since I was a little girl. When I pictured what my mom would've been like, I always imagined my mom's face with Marie's gentle personality. Marie treated me like I was her own. I would always be grateful for her.

Sitting in my marketing class, my mind drifted in and out of the lecture. I really needed to focus or else I would certainly fail.

My phone beeped silently. I took it out of my purse and saw that Chad had sent me a message.

Chad: *Baby love!!!! I got your male model!!!! FINALLY! He's über hot!!! It's going to be FABULOUS!!! Just you wait, love! I'll text you the deets for the shoot next week. I think we'll be doing a shoot once a week for six weeks? I'll let you know! Love You! xxxxxx*

Ha! I wondered where he'd found his model. I just hoped his shots wouldn't be raunchy or tasteless. How comfortable would it be to pose almost nude with a stranger? This should be interesting. I might need to take my accomplice, Don Patron, with me to soothe my nerves.

I just might.

By the time the class ended, it was already six p.m., so I rushed home to cook dinner because I was feeling ravenous. Hopefully, Lucy hadn't arrived yet so I could cook before she did. She usually came home around seven from school. She's a sophomore and had a bad schedule.

When I opened the apartment door, I was surprised that there was noise coming from the living room. *Luce is home early*, I thought.

"Luce? I'm home! What do you feel like for dinner? I'm cooking!" I called out to her as I placed my purse on the floor and checked the mail that was stacked on the rustic-looking table where we placed our keys and other knick-knacks.

I barely glanced up as Lucy came to greet me. She looked a little frazzled which was unusual coming from her.

"Luce?" I gave her a questioning look, but instead of responding, she dragged me to her bedroom and gently closed the door behind me. *Okay...*

"Mrs. Matthews is here!" Lucy exclaimed.

I gasped. *What! Kyle's mother? Here? What in the world is she doing here? Shit! Did something happen to Kyle?*

"Is Kyle okay? Did she mention what she wanted?" I asked dramatically. All these weird scenarios popped and flashed about in my head; none of them any good.

"I don't know. She never said. She's been waiting for twenty minutes. You should go and ask her yourself.

Whatever it is she came here for, be strong." Luce gave me a hug and squeezed me tightly.

"Right. Thanks for the warning." My hand sought out hers, gently squeezing it before I left and strolled towards the living room to find Marie.

My hands were clammy and I rubbed them on my jeans as I entered the living room.

I found Marie gracefully sitting on the couch, drinking tea as she watched the news on the television. I was relieved that Luce had taken care of her and had made her feel comfortable.

"Marie?"

"Sienna, dear, how are you? It's so good to see you again. I was a little miffed that you didn't come to see me when you went back home. I've missed you."

Oh, my. That made me teary and wobbly. I wanted to see her, but the thought of Kyle had stopped me. I didn't know how he would feel about me going behind his back and visiting his mother.

"I'm sorry. I meant to see you, but circumstances made it difficult for me. I've missed you, too."

She stood in front of me and gave me a loving hug. "I hope you're doing okay, Sienna?" She eyed me with concern.

"I'm fine. Is everything okay? You're visiting London?" I cautiously asked her. I needed to know the purpose of her visit.

Marie started to sit down and I sat across from her on the other couch. I needed as much distance between us as possible because it just had to be that way from now on. As much as I like Marie, she's still Kyle's mother and she would look out for her son first and foremost.

"Sienna, let me explain my visit and I hope that you will let me finish before you voice your thoughts. Is that okay with you, dear?" I nodded and said yes, eager for her to get on. "I know it's been extremely tough for you and Kyle both since you moved here. I saw his despair when you left. It tore my heart to pieces to see him go through something like that, but he somewhat survived that hurdle and started to live life again. Since the moment he saw you back home, he's been spiraling out of control and I need to intervene before things really get out of hand and he ends up dead somewhere."

I gasped. *Kyle? Why do you do this to yourself?*

"A few days ago, I caught him passed out in the bathroom with lines of cocaine next to him. I was hysterical with worry and so I called Chris, panicking. We discussed what we needed to do to help our child cope with his problems. We sat Kyle down the next day, after he recovered from his binging." She gently wiped a tear that had escaped her teary eyes. "We asked him what was going through his head and told him how negligent he had been with his actions. He didn't talk much—as expected—however he laid out essential facts of how he felt like 'he's dying inside.' I just wish he would've spoken to me about it sooner. He chose to bottle it all in.

"Instead of putting him in rehab like most people do, Chris and I agreed that it would be best to send him here, to be around you again. You give him perspective, dear, but most of all, my son listens to you. He'll be assigned to scout as well as supervise the UK branch, and at the same time, he can try to see you to make amends. Even if you two don't get back together, you kids should remain friends. You darlings were inseparable and it's painful to see a long standing friendship fall apart.

"Sienna, I know this is asking a lot of you, but I'm asking you a favor—for the first time—to please help my son get better. I'm not sure if this will help, yet I feel that this all started with you. I have no doubt in my heart that you can help him get better if he saw you again. He always listens to you. He loves you."

I was speechless. Kyle coming and living here? Me helping him get better? That's a big responsibility! *How the heck will I handle that? I'm freaked out! So much for cleaning out my closet of emotional baggage!* It was going to drive me mental.

"Marie, how do I even begin? That was a lot to take in. Has Kyle agreed to this? Does he know? When is he coming anyway?"

"He does and he's arriving tomorrow afternoon," she said calmly.

I stared at her in shock, her statement sinking in. *Holy fuck! Kyle will be here tomorrow? What the hell am I going to do? What about Blake?* He'd either go ballistic or understand. Who knew which one, though?

This was all so frustrating. Marie was precious, and she's only ever been kind to me since I moved in with the Brown's. I couldn't let her down without putting up an effort.

"All right, I can try. I'm not making promises, but I'll try."

"Oh, Sienna, thank you! This means so much to Chris and me. Thank you! Kyle will be so happy!"

I don't know about making Kyle happy, but I'll be a friend. He certainly needed to redirect his goals. Deep down, I knew I couldn't see someone so dear to me spiral out of control, either. It was Kyle and he needed me—his best friend, not the lover—and I would be there for him.

Marie stood up and took something out of her purse. She sat next to me and handed me a key. "Here is the apartment key. He'll be staying in the company house in Hampstead. Here's the address and my phone number, just in case you need to call me. Never hesitate to call me, dear. I'm here for *you,* too. I'm simply helping Kyle settle in the apartment and I will be leaving Sunday morning. I was hoping we could all grab lunch or dinner Saturday? Would that be okay?"

"Yeah, that's fine, Marie." *Maybe?*

"Thank you again, Sienna. I'll see you in a couple of days. Have a good night, dear." I nodded as she stood up to leave and then I guided her to the door in a daze.

After she left, I scurried to my room. My palm was holding Kyle's apartment key, a business card with Marie's information and the address of the apartment. I looked down and stared at it, blankly until someone knocked. I looked up as the door slightly opened.

"Can I come in?"

"Oh, Luce! Kyle is going to live in London for a while. They sent him here. They think I can help him get better." My voice was small, but obviously freaked out.

"Are you okay with that? Will you be able to help him without getting too attached?" Her blue eyes studied me as she tucked a strand of her blonde hair behind her ear.

"I don't know. We'll just have to wait and see, I guess."

She nodded and sat next to me on the bed. "I sort of heard the conversation. I was in the kitchen. I didn't mean to pry, but, love, Kyle needs your help. You just have to be the bigger person and set aside any ill feelings for him. This could be tough; although, you're the bravest woman I know and whatever happens, never think that you don't have anyone to speak to. I'm here for you, *always*." I gave her a hug and thanked her for all her support. She then got up to leave me with my daunting thoughts.

It'll be fine, I tried convincing myself.

I was beyond exhausted as I made my way to the kitchen to make a sandwich for dinner.

I didn't want to think anymore. I'd think about my problems tomorrow.

When I went to bed, I slept like a log. I had no dreams, no interference.

Eighteen

I was contemplating what to wear for my date with Blake when I received a text message.

Kyle Matthews: *I'm here. I'll see you tomorrow.*

I sighed. *Way to dampen my mood for my date tonight, Kyle!*

My heart was beating erratically against my chest. I had never been in this position—where I had to deal with an ex while starting to see someone new. This was all so new to me and it was driving me insane. *Should I tell Blake? I really should.* Sooner or later Lucy might mention it to both of the guys and I'd be grilled for information. I knew back in the day they were all curious about him and knowing how Lucy was, she'd probably invite him over for dinner to bond with the guys. I cringed at the thought. *God, please, no.* That would be an epic disaster. Blake and Kyle in the same room would be chaos.

Browsing through my closet, I chose an embroidered, black lace, short cocktail dress and paired that with my classic red Prada, gladiator platform heels. I artfully pinned my hair up and minimized my eye shadow. I was heavy on mascara and my engine-red lipstick. Spritzing my favorite perfume, my phone buzzed as if on cue. It was Blake letting me know that he was downstairs waiting for me. Grabbing my purse, I headed downstairs to meet him.

Coming out of the elevator, I could see Blake leaning lazily against his Aston Martin in a sharp, black suit against a white dress shirt. He looked dashing, sexy and still blindingly sinful. I felt lightheaded all of a sudden. I came out of the building as I heard him whistle loudly, clearly praising my look.

Boy, how I've missed him. I had forgotten how he made my heart pitter-patter like crazy. I was breathless. I went over to him as he pulled my hand and twirled me around with full appraisal.

I smiled like an idiot. "Like it?"

"Like it? I love it, poppet! You look ravishing! That dress certainly had you in mind," Blake said against my lips before he kissed me tenderly. I simply melted. A good whiff of his scent had my body into a lustful frenzy. *Relax, stupid body!*

"I've missed you, my sweet."

"Missed you, too, Blake." I gazed back, my emotions all over the place. I felt so much for him. Things I couldn't explain. I swallowed hard.

"Come on, I don't want us to be late for our reservation."

~S~

Blake took me to OXO Tower Restaurant and Brasserie on South Bank that overlooked the River Thames. It was al fresco during the summer time and I relished the warm atmosphere around me. I had never been there before and the view was beautiful, even more so since I was sitting directly across from it.

I grinned at him.

He smiled back, eyes glittering in the night. "What do you want to drink? Champagne?"

"I think I'll have a watermelon martini tonight."

"I'll order us a bottle of red as well," Blake concluded as he browsed through the menu. He did love his red wines.

Our waiter came and took our order. I let Blake decide what to order for my entrée and he happily obliged. With our drinks in hand, I sipped an ample amount of my martini, closed my eyes and savored the taste. Hell, it was glorious. The decadent drink had just the right amount of vodka, zest and freshly squashed watermelon juice. Delicious!

"Do you always close your eyes when you revel in something you like—food, alcohol, *sex perhaps?*" Blake murmured in a low, husky voice. It was his 'fuck me' voice. *Gah! Why are my nipples hardening?*

My eyes quickly snapped open. Blake was relaxed against his chair with his hand on the stem of his wine glass, his dynamic eyes burning into me. *Damn it, those eyes will be the death of me. I swear it!*

Does he know how fascinating he looks? How every single thing he does makes him even more desirable? Does he notice the other women staring at him longingly? Because I fucking do and I don't like it one bit; especially when we're out on a date. Will I ever manage to get used to his dark beauty? I wish.

Clearing my throat, I murmured, "Yes, savoring them makes you appreciate all the good things in life." The coy smile I gave him made him smolder.

"Yes, I definitely agree. How was your week? How was school? Any news?" *Tricky, those questions,* I thought as I weighed my options.

I swallowed slowly. *Any news?* That seemed a little loaded. "School's good. I like my classes this semester. News? Let see—I'll be modeling for Chad. He's going to have a show in a couple of months."

"Model? *How?*" He looked perplexed.

Okay... I know I'm not model material like the ones he's used to, but at least have the decency to look pleased.

"His theme is Sensual Grunge. He's hell-bent on having me be his model. Go ask him." My voice small and a little hurt because his reaction had definitely wounded my pride.

"*Sensual Grunge?*" the blasted man reiterated.

"Yeah, whatever," I said, shrugging off his annoying attitude.

Blake became quiet, and after a few minutes, his mouth was still shut. *Damn him!* He always did this and it was incredibly uncomfortable. So, instead of glaring at his form, I opted to look about, glancing around at the people milling around with friends, laughing and drinking. Some chatted happily whilst eating their dinner. Everyone seemed to be having a great time except for our table. Biting my lip, I contemplated my news about Kyle. Since he was already in a gloomy state, I thought I might as well drop the bomb.

"Since we're on the subject of news, I just learned yesterday that Kyle's temporarily moving here for work." I took a long sip of my martini.

"Kyle? Matthews? He's here?" His reaction was disbelieving. *Yep, my ex is definitely here in London town.*

"Yes, Kyle is here. He just flew in today."

"Bollocks! I can't believe this! This night keeps getting better and better!" Blake said as he raked his hand through his hair. I didn't get the chance to respond, though, because the waiter laid our food out on the table.

Blake seemed eager to ignore me after that and so I let him. His brows furrowed as he worked on his meal. *What was he thinking?* He looked like he was working something out, but wouldn't voice anything to me. It was so frustrating!

I had a hard time not choking on my meal. His forbidding attitude didn't put me at ease and when the waiter came to clear our dishes and offer dessert, he immediately declined, stating clearly that we were in a hurry.

My stomach dropped.

He hurriedly paid the bill and led us both to the elevator, barely touching my back as he ushered me in. When we got out of the building, instead of walking towards the car, he surprised me and suggested that we walk for a while. He seemed so distant and I couldn't seem to reach him while we walked.

When we stumbled upon a garden, I sat on the concrete bench, waiting for him to say something, anything. The silent treatment was killing me.

"Blake?"

His faced away from me, looking over the clearing that led to the river. The garden was dimly lit, however it wasn't dark enough to hide Blake's stony face. When he finally turned around and faced me, hands in his pockets, his face was completely passive.

What was going on with him?

"Are you going back to him?" he asked, but it sounded like an accusation.

"What? No! I never said I was! I mentioned it because you had to know, even though I'm not going back to him. I can't freely date you at the moment. He'll go ballistic if he finds out. I guess all I'm asking is if you could understand where I'm coming from? Kyle's been through a lot lately and he needs my help. His parents seem to think I'm the only one that can pull him out of this rut. They think I can help him somehow… heal, I mean."

"*Heal him*, Sienna? That's a load of rubbish!" He cursed loudly as he kicked a stone next to his foot. Blake turned his back on me again and sat on his heels, both hands gripping his hair.

I pressed my lips together, knowing I was asking a lot of him, but I had to help Kyle. He didn't have anyone else. I owed Kyle this; at least, no matter what he had done for me we were friends for much too long to turn my back on him.

I stared at the man before me who looked conflicted and I honestly didn't blame him. I would have been, too, if our situations were reversed.

I picked at my nails, antsy and nervous when he got up and turned around to face me again. "Sienna, as I badly want you, I can't fall back and watch on the sidelines as you spend time with him. I can't fathom the fact that you'll be spending time with him, especially after what he put you through! However it's your decision and I fully accept that. He's obviously still significant to you and I understand that, as well. You still love him and that's something I can't compete with. I have to give you up, make things easier for us both.

"We'll still be friends, never doubt that. I'll always be here for you, but what transpired between us this past week is something we should bury and move past." *No! How can he say such things?* I wanted to argue, but his eyes were grim and his lips pressed into a thin line, showing me how serious he was.

My eyes were brimming with tears as I watched him speak. He looked fine, although his voice was something else entirely. He sounded hollow and empty. I knew, deep down, even if I begged him to change his mind, he wouldn't. He had already made up his mind about Kyle and me.

The big question is, how am I going to move on with life after Blake? Yes, he's still planning to be my friend and we could mend things, bring them back to as they were before, yet how will I forget how Blake's kisses make me feel? How will I bury these memories I have of him? I felt tormented with emotions and I had a hard time speaking.

"Are you sure you want to give up whatever it was between us, Blake?" I pleaded, my voice a mere whisper.

"It's not easy for me to say this, Sienna. You know that. " *Do I really know it? I'm not so sure I do.*

I nodded, not wanting to argue his moot point. I unceremoniously got up and walked towards his parked car. There was no point in staying longer in the park, pondering ways to convince Blake to change his mind. It was a done deal in his head. He'd probably concocted this while he had sipped wine and concentrated on his dinner.

The ride back home was silent. He didn't even bother to turn on any music. *What a great night this turned out to be*, I thought bleakly. How I wished things were different, but Blake was obviously willing to just walk away—without much ado—so I would do the same and not dwell on it. Apparently, it didn't mean that much to him so I guess it was time to let bygones be bygones.

He parked outside my building without even bothering to look at me. I stared at him for a bit, waiting for him to say goodnight, but he didn't budge. I hesitantly leaned over toward him, gave him a peck on the cheek and hurriedly left the car. The tension was stifling and I needed to get out of there before I broke down.

The apartment was dark and silent. Lucy usually stayed with Toby during weekends and I welcomed the eerie silence. Not bothering to turn on the lights, the moonlight barely slithered through the windows as I made my way to the kitchen and helped myself to a huge glass of wine.

I'm not going to cry, I willed myself. It was stupid and we had barely started anything; it was too new for it to be significant.

I went to my bedroom and slowly took my shoes and dress off. I took the pins out of my hair, letting it cascade down my naked back. Wearing only my thong, I went to turn on my music and played "Ain't No Sunshine" by Eva Cassidy. Placing it on repeat, I crawled into bed, curled up, alone with my heavy heart and my disgruntled thoughts.

I never did cry.

That night, I dreamt of silks, candles and a pool full of rose petals.

Nineteen

Morning couldn't come soon enough as I stretched lazily on my bed. I reached for my phone and checked for the time; it was ten in the morning. I sighed. I would be meeting Kyle and Marie later today.

How exhausting is this? It drained my soul until I was insipid and lifeless.

I wish I could have danced with Chad today, but Saturdays were usually busy for him at the studio and I couldn't cut it close to dinnertime. I needed enough time to get ready. So I settled for some stretching and a twenty-minute Pilate's session in my living room.

Blake never texted or called last night; it was just as well. He was serious about his decision and I had to let it go. All I had to do now was gather up my courage and my armor for when the time came that Blake decided to bring a date when he was hanging out with us. I flinched inwardly at the thought of those strong hands on another woman. It had never bothered me before, yet since things did happen between us; it was going to be difficult to revert to the old ways. I knew how those hands felt, how great they could make me feel. Alas, it was over and I simply had to move past it.

I did some laundry, dusted and cleaned the apartment. Before I knew it, it was five in the afternoon. I had received a text from Kyle earlier stating where and what time we'd meet. I still had an hour and a half to get ready before I needed to meet them.

I decided to run a bath and soak for fifteen minutes or so before I started getting ready. Browsing through my closet, I decided on another black dress, strapless, short and fitted with an A-line skirt paired with black stiletto heels. I kept my long hair down, reaching a few inches above my butt. Pearl studs finished my look perfectly. Aiming for the classy look couldn't be accomplished properly without pearls, or so they said.

Hailing a black cab on a Saturday night could be very difficult; however, I was fortunate enough that I didn't have to wait long on the pavement. The traffic was terrible, but I was lucky to arrive a few minutes past seven at The Dorchester Hotel in Park Lane. Marie loved French cuisine and I was meeting them in one of the five-star restaurants inside.

Entering the hotel's foyer, it was hard not to miss Kyle. He was standing idly in the corner. His face lit up when he saw me as I passed the glass doors. He was wearing black from head to toe; black dress shirt, jeans and dress shoes.

He immediately sauntered towards me. "Sienna."

"Hello, Kyle." I greeted him as he gave me a light hug, pulled back and inspected me quite thoroughly. His eyes even glinted.

He looked like he had lost a lot of weight since I had last seen him. He had dark rings under his eyes and his skin looked paler. He continued to look handsome, but his usual luster was missing. I felt a jab of guilt looking at him. Deep down, I knew it wasn't my fault that he was having such a rough time; he did it to himself and he should have known better, although the fact that somehow I was a major factor to his spiraling downfall, made it quite difficult for me not to feel some remorse.

"Mom's already seated inside. I just wanted to wait and meet you out here. You know, merely making sure you were coming." *He doubted it?* I would've thought Kyle would know I could hardly say no to his mother.

"I said I was. I wasn't planning on canceling at the last minute." He nodded and led the way to where his mother was located.

Marie looked beautiful in her usual Oscar de la Renta suit in light pink as she greeted me warmly and sat next to Kyle. I sat across the table and Marie immediately took the uneasiness of the situation away. She never once discussed Kyle's problems; instead she directed the conversation towards her charity work and other subjects that she deemed safe throughout the entire meal.

Sipping the excellent red wine, I was a little guarded when Marie's questions turned to an inquisition of my time in England; in her gentle manner, of course. "So dear, tell me about your life here? Is it what you dreamed it to be?"

Smiling, I relented, "I really love it here. I've made my own friends and I'm very comfortable now. School's great, actually! I'm loving where my professor is going with our Art History class. So, I guess I'm happy, if that's what you wanted to know." I took another huge sip of my wine and glanced at Kyle. He seemed a little aloof and engrossed in his phone messages.

"Anyone special, dear?" Marie lightly inquired. Even in her gentle voice, I knew she was dying to know this.

Kyle even managed to pause his tapping on his phone, though he never looked up. I could tell he was waiting for my answer as well.

Mother and son, working together. *Great, this is just what I need. Since I'm not seeing Blake that way anymore, I guess there's nothing to tell them.* Shaking my head, I answered, "No, no one at the moment."

"That's excellent!" Marie exclaimed with a huge smile.

Excellent? Yeah, right.

Marie suddenly stood up and announced that she was off to bed. Her flight was early tomorrow morning and she needed all the rest she could get. She thanked me and kissed me goodnight before doing the same with Kyle.

Now, it's just us, even better.

I fished for my phone and saw that Luce had texted me.

Luce: *Going out dancing tonight! Want to join us in Mahiki? Toby wants to take his friend from work. Say you'll come!*

Oh, definitely!

Me: *Yep! Meet you there in an hour or so!*

I immediately invited Chad to meet us as well, if he didn't have plans already. However, knowing him, he'd probably drag his date to come party with us.

"What's making you smile like that?" I looked up and clashed with his golden-hazel eyes. I hadn't realized he was done texting his friends and giving me all his attention.

Brooke perhaps?

"My flat mate, Luce, just texted me to see if I wanted to go clubbing with them." Putting my phone down next to my glass, I took another copious sip.

"Going to join your friends?" Kyle inquired.

"Quite possibly, yes."

"Can I invite myself as well... If you go?" He picked up my phone and toyed with it. He was acting like the old Kyle I'd known. I was relieved that he was still there, somewhere.

"Shouldn't you be resting? You just barely got here. Besides, after the crap that you pulled with your binge drinking and drugs, going out to party should be the least of your worries, no?" I enlightened him, quirking up a brow with my question. I was furious that he placed himself in harm's way. He could've easily overdosed and died. *What the heck was he thinking?*

"I'm off that, Sienna. It was a deal I had with my parents. I know it's stupid, but I needed to numb the pain I was feeling. I didn't want to deal with it. I took the coward's way out, but now I'm here and I can see you again; not somewhere far away from you. I'm not going to rebel and act out." Handing my phone back to me, he informed me, "You have a message."

It was from Chad saying he'd be on his way soon and he couldn't wait to see the gang.

Chad started hanging out with us the moment Luce and I became friends as well. I was glad that everybody got on, even Toby and Blake liked him. The guys didn't seem to mind that Chad was gay and I adored them for it.

"You're not really seeing anyone, baby?" Kyle finally managed to ask the stupid question I knew he was dying to ask. *Why does he keep studying me? Can't he look away, just for a second? It's making me nervous.*

"I'm not yours to call baby, not anymore." I shot him a hateful glare.

"We'll see, baby."

Huh! *Confident, aren't we?* If he thought I was just going to fall back and be with him again, after he cheated, because he was here in London, he could think again!

The big question is, should I invite him to go to Mahiki and meet my friends? He's eager to go, but what if Blake's there? Nah, he's busy with that Marbella project, remember? Hopefully, Lucy and Chad won't be bothered by Kyle? They might not like him; however, I know they won't be hostile, either.

Draining the rest of my wine, I glanced at Kyle. His eyes were staring at my boobs. I rolled my eyes. I knew the tight dress emphasized my small waist, but it pushed my breasts up—and they looked insanely good. I suppose that's why I'd chosen it. I'd wanted to rub what he'd thrown away in his face. Kyle's a boob man and he loves those suckers. Too bad he wouldn't be doing much with them other than staring at them longingly. I ignored his blatant mishap of calling me 'baby' after I'd rebuked him about it.

"Still want to come and meet my friends?" I double-checked. This was a big deal for me, although I didn't show it. This was going to be the first time my London friends would meet him. It was a major deal.

"I definitely do." Kyle nodded, responding with certainty.

"'Kay, I'm going to refresh my make-up. Lobby in five minutes?" He nodded as I walked away from our table.

Twenty

I was thankful when the cab finally stopped outside the club. The silence in the cab had been deafening. *Awkward much? Why is he acting so weird, anyhow?*

As instructed by Luce, all I had to do was mention Toby Watson to get in right away. I was sure Toby had made reservations before coming here. Count on him to always be prepared. When it came to his ladylove, he didn't think twice about giving her anything.

Have you seen those couples that were toothache-inducing, sickly sweet to each other? *Yep, that was them.* They look like they're made for each other; therefore people tend to forgive them for that.

Brushing past the bouncers, I scoured the booths to look for my friends. I was quite nervous because I hadn't mentioned bringing Kyle. I merely hoped that they would all get along so it wouldn't be completely difficult. Kyle didn't have many friends here, so he was most likely going to follow me about. *God, I hope not. He'll find friends soon enough,* I convinced myself.

The music was thumping and blaring loudly. The place was starting to get packed as more alcohol-induced bodies swayed to the beat on the dance floor. A Polynesian theme was throughout the entire club. It was done tastefully with a touch of contemporary design. This place was known for their exotic cocktails and mixers that came with a fire exhibition. It was quite riveting and the crowd went rampant with awed fascination.

Kyle's hand found my waist as he pulled me in and whispered into my ear, "I think I found your friends. They're all staring, just to give you a heads up."

I quickly turned to my right, away from the fire exhibition, and found their table was actually on the far right, away from the commotion. Kyle was right; they were all staring. I didn't get to check out everyone at the table because I looked down, a little embarrassed as I made my way towards them.

"Sienna Richards, glad of you to grace us with your sexy self," Chad drawled in his flamboyant New York accent. "And you must be?" The question was aimed to Kyle. I totally forgot to mention his move here to Chad. He was going to devour the drama. He lived for these things.

"I'm Kyle, Sienna's friend from LA," Kyle introduced himself to both Chad and Luce then flashed them both his seductive smile. Even tired, he could still manage to look handsome. Kyle had always been handsome in a lean, muscled, surfer, rugged kind of way. His dark hair and his hazel-golden eyes amplified his good looks.

"*The* Kyle?"

"Yes, Chad! Now drop it, please." My eyes glared at him full-on, begging him to stop, but it seemed he didn't get the damn message. Was he drunk already?

"My, my! Don't you two look like the perfect couple! Don't you think, Luce? Toby? Sam? *Blake*?" The moment Chad said *Blake*, my eyes shot behind Chad and looked over the booth. Sure enough, the prince of brooding was sitting conveniently behind Chad, blocked from my view earlier.

Oh, fuck.

Blake looked composed and impassive, as though it didn't bother him. When our eyes met, he simply nodded to acknowledge me and returned to chat with another man I had never met before. *Ouch.* I hadn't seen it coming. He had moved on. Blake's reaction, or what little of it he'd shown, proved to me how over me he was. The dull ache in my chest wouldn't subside, so I ignored it and pretended I was perfectly happy.

Luce introduced Kyle to the rest of the guys and the stranger named Sam. They all seemed nonchalant. Toby and Blake, even less thrilled. I understood the reaction from Blake, *but Toby?*

Kyle's phone flashed and he texted quickly as he pulled on my waist a little too possessively—*directly in Blake's line of sight*—and told me that he needed to make a phone call outside. He quickly kissed my cheek before retreating into the crowd and out the exit door.

My eyes landed on Blake's. From the murderous look he gave me, I didn't have to guess if he'd seen the exchange. His nostrils flared, his jaw muscles tightened and his beautiful eyes screamed bloody murder. Unable to stand the burning heat of his stare, I turned around quickly.

Luce handed me a blue colored drink and Chad pulled my hand, cornering me on the mirrored wall. "You better start explaining yourself, baby love, before I start hyperventilating. Aren't you dating sexy Blake?" Chad rattled on, his ebony eyes curious.

"Blake decided it was best to end it last night when he found out that Kyle's parents had agreed that I'm the medicine for his sobriety—hence the attendance of the one and only—I wasn't expecting Blake here. He's supposed to be busy with a project."

"Goodness! This is awesome drama! I *love* it! It must be wretched to be you right now, huh? How are you holding up?" As quickly as his eyes lit up to the prospect of fireworks, it immediately vanished when he realized how rotten it was for me.

"Yeah, it's fucking dreadful! But, please, let's not talk about it; not tonight. I want to have fun! Is that okay with you, mister?" I gave him a quick hug and kiss on his glossed puckers.

I sat next to Toby and he immediately gave me a tight hug. "Ex-boyfriend coming after you it seems?" I shrugged, not wanting to reply. "If you need anything, don't hesitate to call me. It's not that I don't trust him, but I want you safe is all." He kissed my forehead and got up to join Lucy on the dance floor. They looked so happy together that it made me feel worse.

Taking a sip from my blue sweetened vodka concoction, I noticed Blake toying with his glass of whiskey; possibly contemplating if he should talk to me or not.

"Not busy with the Marbella project tonight?" I asked, leaning a little closer to him.

"Back with him *that* quickly?" Blake's sarcasm was palpable. Didn't I explain the situation last night?

"No, I am not."

I looked around and scouted for someone to rescue me, however it seemed everyone had dispersed to the dance floor. Picking up on my nervous state, Blake leaned close, *so close* that I could smell him. My stomach nose-dived as I closed my eyes and breathed him in.

Damn you, I silently cursed.

"You look bewitching, my Sienna. I seem to recall how well your body responded to me and I'm getting hard thinking about those lips of yours." His gaze went south, gritting his teeth. "Your boobs are indecent. Did you do that purposely to torment and torture me?" *My, God! I love it when he talks dirty.* His cool and composed façade slipped off and another man surfaced.

"If you are tortured and tormented, you have yourself to thank," I managed to whisper as I looked him straight in the eye.

"Seeing how cozy you two are made me think twice about my decision. Do you know how it makes me feel seeing you together?" Even with the loud thump of music his voice was clear and grating on my delicate ear.

"I didn't know you'd be here. If I had known, I wouldn't have come."

Blake abruptly pulled away from my ear and looked over to my side as Kyle came into view. He didn't seem to notice the tension between us or he was doing a good job at pretending not to see it.

Releasing a sigh, I turned to Kyle. "How did your call go?"

"It's good." He gave me a sideways glance and his usual flirty smile. When I stood up, he held out his hand. "Dance with me, baby."

"I don't think that's a good idea. How about we just stay here, hmmm?"

"Come on, baby! We used to have fun dancing! Please? Just this once?" He was still holding out his hand and smiled like an idiot as I took it.

"Fine."

"I'll be right back," I addressed Blake, but he just stared at me, infuriated.

"By all means, dance your socks off," he bitingly responded.

That I will, just you wait.

Joining the crowded floor with people bumping and grinding, Kyle took the opportunity to pull me close to his chest. Our eyes immediately locked and out of the blue he yelled, "I love you."

My mouth opened and closed again. I rotated myself and placed his hands on my waist while we continued to dance, which relieved me from having to talk to him. He seemed to love having his hands on me. His grip was getting tighter as he ground himself a little too close for comfort on my ass.

How did one balance an ex and a "possible" new man in her life? It was Kyle's first day here and I was having a hard time already. I hated what he'd done, and at the same time, I wanted to help him, however it was evident that he wanted more than that. With Blake, though, where did I even begin? He was incredibly baffling. Holding our rhythm, I was starting to have fun dancing with Kyle. We both relaxed and started to enjoy each other. When the music ended, I expected us to dance more, but Kyle led me to the entrance door.

Outside on the pavement, he asked me to take a short walk. and I obliged.

Twenty-one

"I'll give you a few minutes and then I'll go back inside. I don't want my friends to worry," I said to Kyle and he simply nodded in agreement.

When he stopped walking, he leaned on a building, closed his eyes and then spoke softly, "When my parents pitched the idea of me coming here, I was happy and scared. I was scared because you might not love me the way I love you; well, not anymore. I was cruel and I can't forgive myself for what I've done to you. If we turn out to be friends like how it was before we started dating, I'll take that in a heartbeat. I'm really thankful that you're even giving me time, but it was hardly a surprise."

Opening his hazel eyes, they were miserable and anguished. "You have such a good heart, Sienna. You're smart, beautiful and brave. When Christy started beating you, I made a promise to myself that I wouldn't dare hurt you, but I did. I broke that promise. You trusted me. You loved me. How could I betray someone I love so much? I was so consumed with anger and hurt that I forgot to think about how I was hurting you. I'm sorry." Kyle started to massage his temples while sadness racked my body.

I walked over and hugged him tight. The mention of Christy Brown's name sent shivers all over my body; that woman was horrid. "I know you are. That's why I can't stay mad at you for long. What you did was painful and I'm hurt. I just wish that you could've told me about what you were going through. Instead, you looked for a replacement to forget about me. That hurt."

"And look how successful that turned out, Sienna. The moment I saw you again, I was a goner. I was invaded by the thought of you. It's always been you, Sienna; no matter how much I try. My heart belonged and will always belong to you," he professed, a little breathlessly.

I looked down and studied my toes. *Why is it painful when he tells me he loves me?* I love Kyle, I do and I guess I'll always love him, but a big part of me wanted Blake. No point in denying myself anymore. I had always been attracted to him and I couldn't pass this chance up or I might regret it for the rest of my life. *Fuck, baby steps.* I wanted him and that's that.

What I felt for him was complex, but as fascinating as he was, I was not going to let anyone trample on my heart. That's one thing I wouldn't compromise. Once was humiliating enough.

"Kyle, I'm sorry. *I really am*, but right now, I'm not in a place where I would want to be in a relationship. There is too much between you and me. I need to step back and think about what *I* want. All my life, I was attached to your hip. I lived and breathed you; I loved you with all of my heart, however you must understand that things changed. It's different now." I looked at the man I used to love with unshed tears.

His thumbs started to wipe the sides of my eyes. "Don't cry, baby. I feel like a total bastard right now.

Please, don't cry." Kyle hugged me tightly. My head was on his torso as he tried to calm me down. He gently stroked my hair and kissed my cheek.

Pushing myself off his body, I folded my arms as I waited for him. "Let's go inside. We've been out for a while now."

He pulled me close to him and draped his arm around me as we headed to the club's entrance where he immediately stopped. "Go be with your friends, I'm going back to the apartment. I was pooped before we came here, but I wanted to spend more time with you. Now, I'm ready to crash."

"All right, it was good to see you again. Be safe."

Kissing my lips gently, much to my surprise, he bade goodnight. "I'll be in touch, baby. I love you." With that, he headed to where several cabs were waiting on the curb.

I waited until he got in a cab before I let myself past the bouncers who were listening intently to our exchange. I smiled, understanding how boring it must be to stand there all night. "Can't say I blame him, love. I would want to spend all of my time with you," one of the tall, bulky men said as I walked past.

Men, I thought amusingly.

My mood took a sour turn when I saw a tall blonde sitting on Blake's lap. *Here's a reality check*. Moments ago, I had been thinking of being with him and now his hands were on that woman's waist as he fed her olives. Barf.

My blood was boiling and I wanted to throw something at them.

"Turn around," Chad whispered behind my back.

"The old Blake lashed out when he saw how you danced with your old lover. She's an old friend of his who just happened to be here with her own party, but as you can see, they're quite engrossed with each other. Don't mind him; I'm sure he's gutted inside. This is his way of coping." Chad looked sorry as he squeezed my shoulder. I didn't even respond to that because I didn't expect it, but why shouldn't I have? *It's fucking Blake we're talking about!* Here was a side of him that I had never gotten to see before.

I was beyond angry; however, Hell would freeze over before I let him see how hurt I was. "He just glanced here—don't look back!"

Ugh. I can't do this. This is beyond pathetic. I am beyond pathetic!

"Take me to the dance floor, lover." I nervously smiled at my friend, offering my hand to him.

"I thought you'd never ask."

Chad's a blast on the floor and, before I knew it, Luce, Toby and Sam had joined the commotion. Chad grabbed another man's attention, so he was dancing somewhere amidst the throng of people. Luce and Toby were dancing and laughing with each other. So, that left me with Sam who was giving me a kind smile. As we danced next to each other, he leaned in and asked, "Where's the boyfriend?"

I laughed. "No, no, he wasn't my boyfriend; an ex is more like it."

Smiling, he leaned in a bit more. "So, what do you do, Sienna? Apart from breaking hearts, that is?"

Ha! If he only knew!

"Well, I'm still in uni, but for the most part, my time is dedicated to breaking hearts here and there, lighting up drama whenever I can." I was laughing and fluffing him up with his own joke. He was certainly easy to converse with. He wasn't handsome, but his kind eyes and demeanor made him likable.

"Come on, love, let's get something to drink! I'm parched!" It was announced by the thirsty Lucy as she tried to catch her breath while she actively fanned herself with her hand.

"Let's!"

The scene at the booth hadn't changed much. The fucking woman still on his lap, but she was now openly caressing his neck and chest from the unbuttoned, midnight blue dress shirt that matched his eyes.

They can go fuck themselves. I could care less.

Ignoring them, Sam poured us both champagne and I gladly took a huge gulp.

Arching her brow with curiosity, Lucy asked Sam and I, "What were you two discussing earlier? I've never heard Sienna laugh like that." Lucy leaned on the table as she eyed us with amusement.

"We were discussing her full-time job as a heartbreaker!"

"Yup! He was telling me how his heart was broken when I turned him down. He wanted a quick shagging in the bathroom, apparently." I even *tsk-tsked*, loving the whole light-hearted banter. "Such a naughty boy you are, Sam!" I added to boot.

Everyone laughed and Luce almost choked on her champagne. Chad appeared out of nowhere, dripping with sweat and a huge smile like he had just won the lottery. "OMG! Did you see how hot that guy was? I must have died and gone to Heaven." He sat next to me and grabbed my champagne glass, emptying the contents.

"Excited much?" I studied my friend who had a sheen of perspiration glazed on his forehead and his face lit up like Christmas.

"I am. Oh, by the way, I meant to tell you, we're shooting on Thursday. So, you better make sure you bring your sexy-fucking-kitten look. You and Troy are going to be Hot! Hot! Hot!" Chad's excitement was bouncing off him.

"Wait, what? You model for him?" Sam looked interested and intrigued.

"Yeah, he's a photographer and he's awesome! He also sort of needs me to do a few stills for his upcoming show which is in—what? Seven weeks?" I squeaked, glancing back at Chad who was busying himself with another glass of champagne.

"Definitely, and Sam, you're invited," he finally managed to reply to Sam, winking at him. *Such a flirt, this Chad!*

"Wouldn't miss it. I want to see the 'sexy-fucking-kitten' look out of curiosity," Sam responded with ease.

I'm sure he did. What the hell did 'sexy-fucking-kitten' look like anyway? I cringed. I've never modeled before. Let alone have it shown in front of everyone and have it dissected for everyone's pleasure. It was mystifying, but I already promised Chad. I couldn't let him down.

"Oh! Don't mind him. I'm sure it's going to be nice and appropriate!"

"Honey, it's going to be far from nice and appropriate! I can see it now!" Chad closed his eyes as he pictured it in his mind. "You're going to be sexual and you'll have that 'fuck me' look. Troy will be doing the same, touching you sensually. It's going to be a feast for the eyes. Carnal and raw."

Christ. I needed a drink. "That Troy better bring it or I'm packing my bags."

"Trust me; he's hot! Though not as hot as you are, Blake!" Why did Chad like to bring Blake into our conversations randomly? Just because the freaking man was almost perfect, didn't mean he wasn't capable of being an insensitive prick! *Stupid playboy jerk*, I thought haughtily.

Blake smiled at Chad's comment before he averted his gaze back to me. He studied me while the woman caressed him, whispering sweet nothings into his ear.

My eyes flickered to the girl. That stupid woman was seriously lapping it up. She was kissing his neck and toying with his hair. I smirked. *Yeah, keep massaging his ego you stupid flirt; it's already massive and unmanageable.*

I looked away in disgust and anger from their display of foreplay.

Honestly, it was stupid. I didn't have the right to be angry.

I honestly didn't.

Twenty-two

Luce and Toby wanted to go home, so we all decided it was best to leave together. It was two in the morning and I was ready to get some rest anyway.

"Want to split cabs? I'll have you dropped off first?" Chad asked.

"She's coming with me. There's something we have to discuss." I looked at Blake agape. What was he talking about? *No, we don't.*

"Oh, boo you!" Chad pouted. "You lovers enjoy the night then." He smiled, showing off his perfect white teeth.

I rolled my eyes. *Seriously, Chad?*

Everyone shuffled to leave, saying quick goodbyes. I looked around expecting to see his "friend;" however, she was nowhere to be found.

"She's not here." *Of course, she isn't.* He probably just dropped her like a hot potato the moment he realized we were all leaving.

Typical.

"What do we have to talk about? I thought you were perfectly clear yesterday. There's no need to rehash it," I seethed, angry at his ever-changing attitude. *Is he bipolar? No, he isn't. He just likes brain-fucking. He's a pro at that.*

"My flat is only a couple of blocks away. Walking it off would be a good idea, unless you don't agree?" He peered at me, hands in his pockets, his tone more serious.

"Walking is fine. I don't want to be confined next to you in a cab." I didn't mean to be snappy, yet it was irritating that he thought he could just bulldoze his way around. He hadn't even had the decency to ask if I wanted to go with him, he'd simply assumed that I would. *Well, I was curious and I would've gone anyway, but all he had to do was ask.*

We didn't speak to each other. I would've bitten his head off with more snarky comments if he'd tried. He stopped outside his building and held the door for me. The man behind the desk looked up. "How do you do, Mr. Knightly?"

"Hello, Scott. This is Ms. Sienna Richards, one of my best friends."

I greeted Scott as we headed for the elevator. He still wasn't really my favorite person, even with the silence from us both the entire walk home. I was still angry and a little disconcerted by his coveting display with the biotch earlier.

Are you sure you aren't just jealous? What if I am, so what? It doesn't change anything.

I was a bit miffed that he'd started this whole thing between us then immediately decided not to pursue it any longer. Now our friendship was hanging in the balance. *I can't stop thinking about his kisses, either. He's incorrigible.*

Riding the confines of the elevator in utter silence, I couldn't help it when I flinched from the pain in the soles of my feet. Even if it had only been a couple of blocks of walking with three-inch heels, it had been murderous. I would have given anything to soak in a hot bath. I sighed loudly and he didn't even bother to turn around to ask if I was okay. *Douche.*

Entering his apartment, Blake flipped a switch and the lights flickered, surrounding the place with a soft glow. It looked too intimate for my liking. *Maybe I should bail and just go home?* My hands were fidgety. My palms were sweaty. *He better start talking before I collapse from a nervous breakdown.*

I stood in the middle of the living room. Memories of the weekend that I'd spent here with him flashed through my mind. *Nostalgia can really dampen one's emotions*, I thought with wry amusement.

Blake went straight to the bar, poured a glass of brandy and gulped the entire contents in one go. Why was he stalling?

I stared at him, hands on my hips, glaring. "Talk."

"Why are you acting this way, Sienna?" His passive tone rubbed me irritatingly. *The nerve! He's acting like a royal, stupid jerk!*

"How should I be acting Blake? With your little display of shenanigans tonight, why are you even *surprised?* You're such an insensitive prick!"

He moved towards me and his scowl deepened. "Are you fucking serious? *I'm* the insensitive one? Were you not the one who brought your ex and danced with him while... while I sat there and watched his hands *all over you*, groping and fondling your body? Right. In. Front. Of. Me." I felt hot all over. His close proximity bothered me and I was having trouble being coherent. "It took every ounce of my power not to smash his face in. I did

that. For you!" Blake's beautiful face contorted with fury. *He even looks hot and sexy when he's angry.*
Damn it, Sienna. Get your head out of the gutter!
"I didn't realize you were watching the whole time," I whispered slowly.
"Well, that's where you're wrong. I watched you like a hawk all night." His face was mere inches away.
My heart's about to jump out of my body, I swear.
Snaking my tongue to wet my lips, I gazed up with a questioning look. "Why? You ended things—"
Raking his hand through his hair, he spoke, "I did and I meant it last night. That's why tonight was difficult. I was jealous and it obliterated me. Seeing you with him, it seriously caught me off guard. I was raving mad, gutted, and I wanted to return the favor by making you jealous." Cupping my cheek with his thumb, he went on, "I'm sorry for being such an arse. I want you; God, help me." His voice wavered. "I want you like no other. Give me another chance?" His eyes were sad and full of remorse as they sought my own.
Damn that cute accent of his. It melts me like a complete moron.
"I'll be busy in Marbella for the next couple of months looking over the project. I'm hoping this will be enough time for you to consider me—us—again?"
I was rendered speechless. *Think. Mind. Think.*
Biting my lip, I found my voice. "Blake... yeah, I think that's enough time for us to weigh in on if we really do want this." Blake beamed happily at me.
I think I've lost all the fight I have in me, all the reasoning my mind can come up with. I wanted to live and feel alive.

"Thank you. You won't regret this, I promise." Blake kissed my forehead... my cheek...

The moment he kissed me, I was done for. There was no possibility of going back. *He's in my blood and I'm fevered. I want him.* He drove me with this tug of constant need. Everything about him, it pushed me into a frenzied state.

"Blake, just fucking kiss me already—"

The instant our lips touched, I was completely and utterly lost. Deepening the kiss, I let out a loud moan. Blake playfully bit my bottom lip and I nipped him back. He continued devouring my lips while I ran my hand through his luxurious hair and I trailed the other down to squeeze his erection. *I wanted him. All of him.*

Blake growled and tore himself off my swollen lips. He swiftly picked me up and threw me over his shoulder; caveman style. I screamed and laughed loudly at his dominating display. "Put me down, you brute!"

He threw me roughly onto his bed. My eyes expanded as Blake crawled predatorily towards me. His eyes were absolutely savage. Kissing my legs, my thighs, my heaving chest, my neck and then locking his lips onto mine again. His kiss was punishing and I exalted from it. I wanted him just as much.

This consuming, driving need to simply *be* with him was distracting.

"You're going to be punished for what you did tonight, my love," Blake harshly bit out. His hoarse tone loaded with promise, passion. My body reacted wildly to it as I became moist at the juncture of my thighs.

My body tingled. "I'd love for you to do it rough—" I moaned to him. Blake moaned my name as he bit my neck, *hard*. I gasped from the pain and ecstasy it brought. My insides quivered with anticipation. I panted as his hand trailed smoothly up my leg.

When he teased the inside of my thighs, he promised, "Ask and you shall receive, milady."

Hands on my waist, he swiftly yanked me to the edge of the bed, demanding. "Turn around. Let me take off your dress. Leave your shoes on." He sat on the edge of the bed, scrutinizing my every move.

Anything, just don't stop. My mind was fogged, my lecherous body enslaved.

Shrugging off the dress, I let it drop to the floor. Stepping aside, I stood before him with underwear and shoes on. His eyes hooded as they gradually took in my half-naked body, caressing it with those beautiful eyes of his. "Come here." His voice was gruff, fervid.

I sauntered back to the man and halted right in front of him. Blake immediately fixated his attention on my breasts, cupping my heavy tits as he savored them. He bit, squeezed and pinched. My head fell back, moaning as illicit pleasure coursed through my body.

Leaving soft kisses as he trailed towards my navel then further south as I arched my back, reveling in the high he was giving me, wanting more. He pulled my flimsy underwear off and instantly cast them aside.

Blake parted my legs and made a rough, throaty groan. "Your cunt is dripping beautifully, my love. *You want me that bad?*" Licking the moisture off with a swipe of his tongue, my body shook as I held onto his shoulder. "Tell me, how badly do you want it?" Blake's demanding tone made me stare at him, agape. He was looking at me, waiting.

I groaned with frustration. "I want you. I've always wanted you. " My confession was rewarded with his sinful smile. I looked at him through my half-lidded eyes as he nipped on the corner of my inner thigh. *Touch me,* my mind screamed. "Show me, Blake. Want me, punish me; I don't care. I—"

I stopped begging as he plunged his tongue inside me. Moaning as he flickered on the nub and inserted a finger inside of me. My body was hot and humming beautifully from his ministrations. My eyes rolled to the back of my head when he inserted another finger. Pulling in and out of me, circling and hooking towards the spot that was critical for my orgasm. *Fuck. Me.* My body quaked and I panted his name loudly.

"Not yet," Blake muttered as he pulled his fingers out. Then he traced his wet digits on my lips and stuck them in my mouth. I sucked them, hard, stroking them with my tongue as if they were his cock. He moaned, eyes loving how wanton I looked before him. "How you drive me crazy, woman."

I pulled his belt and pants down followed by his boxers. I hungered for him, to taste him. *I want it all.* His swollen, enormous cock sprung free and my hand gripped it boldly, greedily. I stroked him slowly and replaced my hand with my tongue, twirling it up and down, wetting him slowly. I gazed at him as my mouth enveloped his length, gradually and precisely until it hit the back of my throat.

"*Jesus!*" He rasped through gritted teeth, fascinated.

Still holding eye contact, I used my tongue and lips to stroke him with ardent speed. He grabbed my head, clutching my hair, pushing me down more. I did as he wished, giving him all I had until he couldn't take it anymore.

He pulled me up towards him and laid me gently on the bed. "I want you," Blake declared as I scratched his nipples with my nails. Growling, he went onto his knees as he parted my legs. He expertly massaged the nub of my mound while I grabbed his cock at the same time, stroking it, sliding it back and forth through my slick, wet folds.

His cock feels fucking glorious! I was dying from pleasure, begging him to take me while he massaged my breast and lightly pinched my nipple. The head of his cock was teasing my entrance. I spread my legs wider, silently begging him to end my sweet, tortured misery.

I moaned his name. "Are you sure about this? I don't want you to regret it. I promised to wait. I want you to be sure," he panted while his engorged shaft teased my opening. I groaned; *this man is killing me.*

"Blake—I want you—please—" I heaved as he inserted his engorged head gently inside of me. I completely stopped breathing. His head was filling me slowly, but his size was much bigger than what I was used to.

Nervous, I clenched my vagina muscles unintentionally. "*Jesus, baby*—Fuck! Don't do that—you're impossibly tight. I might just explode—" His neck veins were showing, straining as he closed his eyes like he was restraining himself, savoring his own sweet agony.

"*Bloody fuck... you feel... so beautiful.*" He inched himself a little bit deeper this time. He folded my legs and pinned them down with his hands, giving him fuller, deeper access. Thrusting his hips as his cock went deeper inside me. He was enormous and my insides were stretched to their capacity, raw, with no room left. I flinched from the pain. He halted as he sensed my discomfort, cock pulsing thickly inside me. "Are you okay? I can stop if you want." I shook my head, urging him on.

"No, no. Don't you dare stop!"

Blake started to move again. I placed a finger on my clit and massaged it. The gesture made me wetter, making it easier for him to glide his cock freely. I moaned as he picked up his thrusting speed, taking everything he could. His speed changed. Blake pounded and pummeled harder. "You like being fucked by me, Sienna?" he questioned as he placed my legs on his shoulder. The arch of my hips made it easier for him to access me with thrusting speed. I moaned his name, urging him to fuck me harder as my orgasm shattered through my body. It came in waves and my convulsing body quivered as he pounded a few more times. He yelled my name through gritted teeth as his own orgasm rocked him, spilling his cum inside me. I clenched and squeezed my muscles, milking him to the very last drop.

We both continued to pant heavily as he pulled himself up on his elbows and looked at me with a huge grin. "That was out of this world, my Sienna." Blake kissed me softly. "Now that I know what it's like with you, I'm never letting you go, *ever*." He kissed me harder this time, full of promise.

Rolling to our sides, Blake gathered me towards him. "Sorry I came inside you... I couldn't help it. Are you on the pill?"

I nodded and smiled at him. "Why?"

"So, I can have you anytime tonight. I'm leaving tomorrow afternoon. I wish I could stay here with you all weekend in bed." I nuzzled his neck as he hugged me closer. Skimming my arm gently, he spoke, "What made you change your mind tonight? I thought you wanted to wait on sex?"

I stiffened from his question, but he had the right to know. "I've always wanted you. From the moment I saw you, I knew I was in trouble. I realized what was at stake—when you walked away from me—" I swallowed. "Regrets can be damning to one's soul. The 'what if' scenario would haunt me forever if I didn't give you a chance to see where this is going to lead." Sitting up, fidgeting on the blanket that I held dearly to my chest, I went on, "I have issues, Blake, with trust and being vulnerable. When Dad died, everything I knew and loved was taken away from me. My home was sold, my friends vanished, love and security was gone... my dad's sister took me in. They didn't appreciate my interruption in their lives. Her husband and daughter both resented my presence in their home."

My voice shook, but I had to keep going. "I was taunted, threatened, beaten up and tortured by all of them. If I was late waking up for school, they would douse me with a bucket of water. When I didn't finish my meal, I was beaten with a shotgun cleaner. If I did something that infuriated them, they made me kneel for six to eight hours on a pebbled floor, sometimes more, only in my undergarments. I got my hair pulled. I was dragged and slapped in whatever way you could imagine." I heaved a heavy sigh. "Never once did I fight back. I was helpless and I was at their mercy. I was seven; it was either live with them or go to social services."

"Didn't any of your teachers know about this? Didn't they notice your bruises?" His voice wavered as he spoke.

"Not in the beginning, but after this one incident, I had a lot of cuts on my legs from the metal shotgun cleaner they'd used. I was bruised badly and the cuts were deep, so the blood gushed profusely. I only had band-aids to cover them, but they weren't big enough. The blood oozed off my legs and stained my socks. That's when the teachers noticed. My aunt and uncle were called in to school, but they negotiated with them, I guess. They had power and money after all. None of the teachers or the principal ever bothered to mention it again."

"When did they stop?"

"Two years ago, when I started dating Kyle and he threatened to report them, but I stopped him. It's not that I don't want to see them pay for what they've done to me, but life has a way of catching up to us and I don't want to live with so much hate in me. Hate ruins people and I didn't want to lose perspective of what I want my life to be like.

"I've forgiven them, but forgetting is another matter. I still get nightmares from time to time, but I won't let them win. I just won't. I'm stronger than that."

Blake hugged me from behind as he whispered softly, "I'm so sorry. I knew you were hiding something, but never once did it occur to me that you were an abuse victim. People who do that to helpless children are sick, twisted human beings. I feel wretched. I want to ease your pain, but I don't know how." His heart was beating erratically on my back. I could tell from his breathing that he was angry. It was a ragged sound.

"Just be here. I don't want to talk about it anymore. It's in the past; let's leave it there." I twisted my head to study his face. Leaning in, I kissed him with all the emotions that were rolling off me.

There were only a few people who know about my past—Kyle, Chad and Lucy. Sharing this part of me with Blake was huge, however I needed him to understand when the time came that I may, most likely, fall short of his expectations. Trust was important and I trusted him as my friend, but as boyfriend or lover, we were still working on that. I may not have offered my heart, yet I could offer him everything else.

"Just promise me one thing," I said against his lips.

"I'll give you anything, poppet."

"No matter what happens, be honest. Promise me that, Blake?"

With his thumb on my chin, he lifted it until my eyes met his silver, midnight blue eyes. All sorts of emotions went through those depths and I was left dumbstruck. The gold flecks stood out and the effect was utterly spellbinding. This gorgeous, enigmatic man had irrevocably ensnared me. "I promise that I will always be honest and never lie to you. From now on, I will protect you as my own. You're mine now; no harm will come to you."

My entire body swelled from his protective and possessive nature. He was a Knightly; it came with the territory, I suppose.

Resting my head on the expanse of his chest, I pondered our conversation. "I had a wonderful childhood," he spoke softly. "My parents were so in love with each other and they both never failed to tell me or show me how much I was loved. When I saw how other parents treated their children, I felt blessed that mine were wonderful. When they died, I was angry because they left me, but at the same time, I was grateful that they were taken together. I don't know how one would have survived without the other.

"Grandfather taught me to have a backbone. To be strong and master my emotions. He once said that once your emotions get the best of you, your rational and logical thoughts erode. A man could be easily conquered, easily defeated, and the valuable idea of focus would evaporate.

"He wasn't easy to live with at first and I rebelled. I was angry at everyone, but I hadn't realized that he was hurting as well. He lost his son, and we were both grieving. We reached a compromise and his constant encouragement along with the reminder of my parents held me in check. For that, I am grateful that he never gave up on me. Grandfather's the only one I have left. I swore to myself that I would never disappointment him."

He paused and stoked my hair. "Sienna, I've never done this before."

I looked up. "What? Having someone on your bed?"

He smiled and pinched my cheek. "No, you beautiful wench; a proper relationship. What I had was a mutual agreement between two consenting adults, exclusive sex with no strings attached. But this, this is different. I need you to be patient; this is all new to me. I'll make mistakes, I assure you; don't condemn me without talking to me first. It's all I ask."

"Thank you for telling me, Blake. You don't know how happy it makes me to hear you say that. I promise, I'll be patient with you."

He left loud, smacking kisses all over my face as I giggled like a little girl who got her wish from Santa. "I can die happy now; I've waited so long. Now, here you are—" kissing my neck and my earlobe "—driving me mad with hunger. You're this burning need in my blood, Sienna, and I'm ravenous." Rolling me on my back, he quickly demolished my lips.

The only thing that was running through my mind was, *mine, he's mine,* as he annihilated my body with voracious greed, quenching his thirst.

His touch was rough and raw, yet the thrill of having him again consumed my very being. When he finally rammed his cock inside with full force, I welcomed it lasciviously. His lovemaking was demanding, hard and harsh like a man starved; I matched his need. There were no words spoken. Our bodies spoke for us.

Never in my wildest dreams had I imagined this soul-consuming connection with anyone. It was a connection that obliterated my sanity. It yearned with no concession. It was like a hypnotic state of a nonsensical, merry-go-round of emotions with no chance in hell of slowing down. People always spoke about it, but I'd never understood their uncontrollable obsession, *until now.*

I was petrified and scared shitless, however I didn't have the capacity to walk away from him.

It was all or nothing.

Twenty-three

"Poppet, wake up," Blake's voice trailed along my neck as it sent goose bumps all over my body. I sighed contently. *I like being woken up like this.* I was on my stomach as he began kissing me across my shoulder and then his kisses trailed lower.

Jesus, the man has more stamina than an Arabian horse.

I was caught by surprise when he swiftly lifted my butt and placed a pillow underneath me. My ass was raised into the air, hailing his undivided attention. His thumb rubbed my clit intensely as he licked the lips around it and stuck his tongue inside my opening. He groaned loudly when I moaned his name. He was insatiable and I loved the fact that he couldn't get enough of me.

If this is his way of marking me, then mark away, lover!

Lifting his body to his knees, he squeezed my ass with both of his hands. He took his sweet time, torturing me with the head of his cock, swiping it back and forth on my clit to make sure I was wet enough.

My mouth hung ajar as I groaned from his ministrations. "Blake! Fuck me already!" I was aggravated and beyond aroused! I wasn't to be me messed with!

Thrusting his huge cock, he penetrated me quite roughly; the sudden impact stunned my body for a mere second. I was a bit sore from his rough handling last night, though my greed for him seized me entirely and erased any thought of the soreness. I moaned as he took himself deeper.

My pussy was salivating from the building pressure. He pulled my hips and commanded me to lift myself to all fours as he pounded my cunt harder. The impact of his balls slapping and hitting my wet folds just heightened my burning need.

He slapped my ass. Hard. I howled from the impact of his palm as I felt a well of liquid seep out of me. My mind went blank from the excruciating hunger that rumbled inside.

"You feel incredible," Blake said in between heavy panting.

Grabbing both of my ass cheeks with his hands, gripping them firmly as he fucked me harder, my body tightened from his animalistic lovemaking. I yelled, gripping the sheets as my body was released from its misery. My orgasm overwhelmed and paralyzed me as his tempo picked up faster than before.

"*This pussy belongs to me,*" he growled loudly through gritted teeth. "Tell me it's mine. Tell me!" his voice roared possessively.

"This pussy's yours, Blake. It's yours. I'm giving it to you. *Take it. It's yours,*" I breathily panted as his orgasm came to a close. With one last thrust, he stiffened and spilled his semen inside me.

He panted heavily, his cheek on the back of my shoulder as he said, "It's mine, all mine; don't you dare forget that!"

Loud. And. Clear.

~S~

After Blake's lovemaking, my lids started to get heavy. I submitted to my body's demand for recuperation as sleep took over.

A loud thud woke me from my slumber. *How long did I nap for?* I sleepily wondered.

I sat up and yawned loudly as Blake entered the room dressed in a black suit, stark white dress shirt and a black silver-patterned tie. My eyes greedily roamed all over him. He looked sharp and utterly delectable. My mouth watered.

And he's leaving for a month and a half. How the hell am I going to survive now? I'll miss him like mad.

The bed dipped as he sat on it, smiling affectionately as he traced my swollen lips with his thumb. "You look flushed and satisfied, my sweet. Your hair's all sexily mussed up and you look absolutely beautiful."

Gazing contently at him, I smiled like an idiot. "Maybe you did something right, Knightly." I suggestively licked my lips, my fingers playing with his hair behind his ear. "Your skills are extraordinary; *incomparable.*"

Every time he smiles at me I feel like I'd just won the lottery. I was such a sucker for his smiles. I was hopeless!

Smiling in between his soft kisses, he managed to say, "Oh yeah? Try to remember that in the next few weeks. I'll try to get away as much as I can, though you have to understand the kind of pressure I have at the moment. I have so much to prove to my grandfather." He paused as his eyes scanned my face. "Just remember how good it'll be when we see each other again."

Yes, it will be hella crazy.

"Blake, everyone that knows you, knows how incredible you are. Your own investments have been phenomenal. I don't doubt you for a second. As for your *other* worries, stop, okay? You're worrying for nothing." I kissed his lips to assure him.

"All right, I have to leave for Gatwick Airport. I hate leaving you here." He took something out of his pocket and handed me a key with an embossed, golden, oriental lily with intricate pink and white diamonds around the designed keychain. It was probably about two and half inches in diameter.

I swallowed.

"Are these *real* diamonds? Blake, this must've cost a fortune!" I stared at him in shock.

He simply shrugged. "You're worth it, poppet."

I looked down at it with confusion as I traced the lily with my finger. Sometimes I tended to forget how loaded Blake was; this keychain cost probably a fraction of his shaving paraphernalia, *but still*. We hadn't properly dated yet.

He knew I loved this particular type of lily. The intoxicating perfumed smell and the contrasting colors of pinks were too beautiful to explain. My insides swelled from the thought that he could remember insignificant details about me.

"This is the spare key to my apartment. I already informed the lobby about you. It's your second home now. I've been meaning to give this to you since you gave me yours, but didn't get the chance to. I know how much you love this particular kind of lily so I thought it would be a nice reminder when you see it, hoping that you'll think of me."

"Thank you! It's very sweet and a thoughtful gesture, however I don't need a reminder of you, Blake... you're in my thoughts all the time."

"Good to know because you're in mine, every second," Blake declared, getting up and kissing me one last time. We said our goodbyes and he left for the airport.

~S~

The apartment was silent without him. I took the pillow he slept on last night and inhaled his scent; lemons and the smell of his intoxicating skin. *Maybe I should take the pillow with me when I go. Tempting.*

I miss him already.

Grazing my fingertip on the lily keychain, I flipped it over and was surprised that he'd had it engraved. Cradling it on my palm, I read it slowly. *"And one by one the nights between our separated cities are joined to the night that unites us."*

I'll be thinking of you, poppet.

It was a quote by the famous Pablo Neruda, one of my favored poets. My heart thudded as I traced the engraving. *He remembers everything that I like!* With his razor-sharp, brilliant mind, I was not surprised that he did.

However the thought of him making an effort is a major deal.

Bubbles of happiness coursed through my body.

He thinks of everything; so far, I'm putty in his hands.

He simply knows how to put a smile on my face.

Twenty-four

Three days had passed and I was still high on Blake and I didn't want it to stop. It was even better than a triple chocolate cake and crème brûlée put together. *Though I'm sure if you put them all together, I would devour them all with gusto.*

We'd been relentlessly calling and texting each other. With the permit problem fixed, there was still much for him to get done. His schedule was punishing, yet he still made time to call me every night before he went to bed. Sweet, wasn't it?

I was walking on cloud nine as I entered the restaurant where I was meeting Kyle for lunch. It was a block away from school, so saying no to him when he'd invited me for lunch had not been an option. He was already at a table and stood up as I approached him.

The dark circles were gone, his face bright and handsome as ever. He was wearing his usual get-up; jeans, shirt and his rugged Timberland boots. He looked well. *I'm glad that his transition in the office had worked out fine.*

"How are you, baby?" He kissed my cheek before I sat down. Kyle had always called me baby, even before we'd started dating. There was some odd sense of security knowing that he was here with me. I suppose it was because he had been a big part of my life growing up.

"I'm good! What about you? How's work?" I asked before taking a sip of water.

"What's this?" Kyle asked as his finger pointed at the folded flyer in my hand. He jovially took it, his long, manly fingers prying it open.

"You're looking for a job? Why didn't you say so?" He peered at me as he popped an olive.

I was staring at his mouth. I looked away quickly, a little embarrassed. *Damn, he's still cute and sexy to boot. Are these normal reactions to your still-hot looking ex? I suppose so. I mean, it was merely a month ago since that mouth went downtown on my body.*

"I don't know what I want yet. Have to see what's available. Although I want to work somewhere challenging, you know, a job that I can learn from and apply later on in life."

"Well, why didn't you say? I'm interviewing for an assistant," Kyle informed me, smiling widely.

"You're joking, right? Why would you *need* an assistant, Kyle?" He usually did his own thing.

"Hey! Don't underestimate my abilities. You know I've been working for the company since I was sixteen. I've earned my position. All I'm saying is that I have a spot available, if you're not interested, too bad." He shrugged slightly as he devoured another olive.

"Sorry, I wasn't underestimating your abilities. I was just surprised. Climbing up the ladder, hmm? I'm happy for you, but as you can see, my class schedule is a little crazy. I don't see how that could work."

The waiter took our order and placed a bottle of red wine and breadsticks on the table. Kyle poured wine in our glasses while I munched on the olives and breadsticks.

I was famished.

"The schedule's going to be flexible. You will be working more at night when I scout during gigs or talk to bands during shifts. You only have to go to the office once or twice a week to do some paperwork. Other than that, you can send emails through your phone when I need you to get some things done."

"Hmmm, are you sure you want me as your assistant, Kyle?" Arching my brow at him, I questioned his sanity. "What if we fight all the time? What then?"

"Baby, you forget that it's me you're dealing with. For years, I've dealt with your PMS and your mood swings." I choked on my olive, but he kept going. "I took care of you when you were sick, held your hair as you puked your guts out over the toilet, taught you how to drive; need I say more?"

"Fine, I get it. When do you want me to start?" I smirked. *I wonder what it'll be like working with Kyle.* He was passionate about his job and I admired that, however there was a lot of baggage between the two of us now.

"How does Friday night sound? I need to check out a band that's playing in Camden."

"Friday sounds bueno! Try not to be such a slave driver, okay?"

I couldn't wait to start work. I had always wondered how it would be working behind the scenes; the process, the thrill of signing a great band. I was dying to know.

"I'll definitely try not to work you to the ground, baby," he murmured softly. *I wonder if Blake will be bothered that he calls me 'baby?'*

Our food arrived and our conversation steered to his job as well as what he had been up to. Stories flowed and we chatted about the people we knew back home. His easygoing personality made it easy for me to be comfortable with him again. If we continued with this kind of progression, our friendship would bounce back in no time. I was confident that it would.

We parted after our lunch date and I had to scurry to The National Gallery Museum to meet my class. Today, we were going to learn about Botticelli and his work. I was energized and psyched that I would get to study it close-up. Last week, I had been awestruck with the works of Jan van Eyck, especially with *The Arnolfini Marriage* illusionism painting. It was simply unique and his perfect execution of geometrical points and perception were outstanding. Not to mention, his application on the reversed reflection of the mirror with immaculate detail had rendered me speechless. His one-of-a-kind depiction of lighting had also made it extraordinary. I had been intrigued and enraptured.

Our class was small with twenty students who were all eager to learn about art and its history. When I got there, the class had already gathered at the far end of Trafalgar Square as our teacher, Mrs. Samantha Collins, checked her roster. She was a charming British lady who talked animatedly with passionate alacrity for anything and everything pertaining to art. Some people had the zeal for it and others were simply apathetic about the subject. I, for one, liked to be absorbed in the artist's craftiness and mastery.

The execution of their imagination in fine, intricate detail was simply gravitating. It was like being transported and seeing it from their eyes. Their hopes, dreams, emotions, their soul and their very being were captured from their compelling, graphic artistry. My ingénue mind was keen to learn and grasp their unrivaled ingenuity.

While studying the *Venus and Mars* renaissance painting, I received a message from Blake.

Blake: *What have you been up to, poppet? Stuck here about to head for a meeting. I'm knackered.*

I couldn't help turning mushy every single time I got a message from him. I smirked when he used "knackered," British slang for tired. I was still learning their British colloquialism, but it was funny how I tended to use some of them now. Chad, too, but he'd been here for almost five years. He came here to study after high school and decided to stay when he graduated. He told me that once you fall for London, it was hard to let go.

I rushed a reply.

Me: *I'm at the National Gallery studying. Btw, I found a job! Drink up some of your beloved espressos. I'm sure that'll help put you back in top form.*

My phone beeped again.

Blake: *You were looking for a job? Why didn't you mention it, poppet? If you ever need money, just say so. Give me your banking details. I'll have it wired to you immediately.*

I almost choked on my saliva.

Me: *No, thank you. Keep your money; it wasn't the issue. I just want to see if I can explore more and meet new people. I only have school and I hate being idle.*

Luce mentioned once a few months ago how Blake would give hefty allowances to his women. A week or a month, it didn't make a difference since he simply spoiled them rotten. Apart from his god-like handsomeness, he was like the Roman god Plutus incarnated, squandering his wealth and lavishing the over-eager strumpets that were ready and willing for him. If Blake Knightly said jump, they eagerly respond, "how high?" *I'm not bitter, much.*

Honestly, I can't recall how many women he'd dated since I'd met him; there were countless of them. It was dangerous to think about. A speck of doubt was a speck of venom that would surely poison our budding relationship. We were still building our trust with each other as lovers; my mind could not wander about in the unchartered territory of doubt.

With Kyle, I had encountered many instances where women hit on him constantly or "friends" that would try to seduce him while I was not paying attention. It was aggravating to say the least. With Blake, though, it was like comparing a gigantic lake to an ocean. Overwhelming didn't even cover it.

So, what's a woman to do? I simply pushed it aside and distracted myself with dancing or with a handful of French and Italian pastries. *Voila! It works like a charm.*

Blake: *Sorry, meeting just started. Which company will you work for? When do you start?*

My stomach did a somersault. *Should I tell him the truth or skirt around it? He'll eventually find out.* It was better to break it to him now rather than later.

Me: *I start tomorrow. I'm an assistant for M.A.T.T. Music. It's off my major, but too good of an opportunity to pass up. I'm pretty psyched about it!*

I hit send before I could change my mind.

My phone vibrated immediately. *Whoa, that was fast. Isn't he in a meeting?*

Blake: *Isn't that Kyle's company? You'll be working for him? Rubbish. Tell him you're going to quit. I'll get you a job somewhere suitable.*

He's not serious? Screw you. He could shove his demands somewhere else. I wasn't budging.

Me: *Don't dictate my life! My mind is capable of making rational decisions. If you're not happy about it, well too bad; deal with it.*

If he's going to think I'll be complacent like his previous women, then he can think again! I shoved my phone back in my purse, infuriated with his attitude. I'd rather get back to studying Botticelli paintings than deal with His Royal Highness.

My phone vibrated again, but I ignored it.

Let him simmer and fester. He deserved it.

Twenty-five
Blake

It had been a hectic day full of meetings, video calls and now, it seemed it was going to get even better. Amelia Mendez was in the middle of her presentation when my Blackberry vibrated. Everyone noticed, but I didn't give a damn. My mood wasn't going to be messed with or they'd end up getting fired. Amelia smiled and proceeded. She'd been giving me a lot of blatant come-hither looks. She was certainly beautiful, but I'd been subtly declining her advances.

I'd turned them all down since Sienna became mine.

Sienna: *Don't dictate my life! My mind is capable of making rational decisions. If you're not happy about it, too bad; deal with it.*

Christ! This woman's impossible! How can she think that working with Kyle would be all right with me?

Me: *I made my feelings perfectly clear concerning that cretin. I'm being rational. I can get you a job anywhere, name it. Kyle has motives. I just want you to be safe; that is all. I miss you, poppet.*

I placed my phone back in my pocket and waited for her reply. Ten minutes passed and she still hadn't. She was obviously ticked off. I'd give her time to calm down.

It was evident to everyone within sight that he wanted her back, but his loss had been my gain. I wasn't as feebleminded as he was. He hadn't realized how special Sienna was, however I did. I'd waited gallantly for almost nine months. I wasn't going to let him snatch her away. *Hell. The. Fuck. No.*

That first night I had seen her at Toby's party, I had immediately been bewitched. She wasn't the type of woman I was usually attracted to, but, Christ, any man would have to be blind not to be captivated by the exotically golden/green-eyed beauty and her lush curves, especially that toned, succulent ass of hers. Her body was just perfect; long wavy mane, C-cups, small waist and a nice rounded, pert bottom. She was the kind of woman who could make a man groan as she passed by. She was lethal to all hot-blooded males in her vicinity.

I was shocked after I had been introduced to her and had made the realization that she was not superficial, instead she was quite a sincere person. She was a breath of fresh air with enough sass, wit and sweetness melded into her goddess beauty that I had instantly wanted to know more about her.

I couldn't get enough of her.

When Toby had seen where my eyes had wandered, he'd warned me to back off. He'd mentioned that she was in a *very* committed relationship with her childhood sweetheart and there was no chance in hell of breaking them up. They were in love and would marry someday. So, I had retreated. How could a man compete with that? Love was anathema to me. I had seen my parents in love, but never had I experienced it for myself.

Yet, I couldn't stay away from her. I was drawn to her; hook, line and sinker. So, I settled for her friendship. When our friendship had flourished, it made me want her more. We had a lot in common and she was fun to be around, but I had to keep my desires buried when she was near. I quietly lusted from afar for months as I practiced the art of restraint and placed a harness on my feelings. When she broke the news that Kyle had cheated and started seeing someone else, I was triumphant and my mind was set on having her.

My plan faltered when she decided to go see him after what he'd done. I let her be. If closure was what she needed, then closure was what she'd get. Had I known at the time what that visit would result in, I wouldn't have let her go.

When Lucy casually mentioned that Sienna was back early, how distraught she was and *why* she was distraught, furious didn't amount to what I'd felt then. The impulse to see her was imminent and I made a dash to my flat to get her spare key. I let myself in the apartment, ready to confront and berate her; however, when I'd opened her bedroom door and had seen her sleeping so soundly, all thoughts vanished.

It pained me that she'd slept with him, but it didn't change the fact that I still wanted her more than ever. I had to tread carefully when pursuing her, though all my good intentions of taking it slowly had vanished when she'd taunted me in the car; when she had spoken in Spanish. I knew the language fluently, but when she purred in Spanish, I had been flabbergasted. I wanted to fuck her right then, yet I did as she asked and waited.

Then, when she broke the news about Kyle moving here and she needed to help him, I was conflicted. I wanted her, but she was still attached to the man. That night at the park, I was at odds with myself. I wanted her; however, I couldn't bring myself to ask if she was still in love with him. If she was in love, how in God's name could I compete with that? I did what I had to do; I walked away. My Sienna didn't make it easy for me, though. She had to drag that cretin to the club and flaunt him as he groped her right before my eyes. Roaring jealousy floored me and ripped me apart. I was done for.

I knew then.

I knew that if I didn't possess her, I would be haunted by her forever. They say life was about taking risks, right? My sanity was at stake; the decision had been made.

That same night, when she finally gave herself to me, something deep inside me had changed.

A soul-shifting alteration that had touched the very core of my being; Sienna had done that, unbeknownst to her.

The meeting ended. I thanked everyone as they departed and scampered back to their offices. Amelia sauntered towards me, placing her hand on my chest; a bold move for a bold woman. I met her three months ago when I made a quick trip down here to oversee the new branch, along with the new project. I was attracted to her and she had easily given in to my advances without hesitation. For two whole nights, I had enjoyed her body. However, seeing her now didn't do anything for me. Although she obviously wanted to pick up where we'd left off.

"Señor Knightly, what time will you need me to be ready for the gala tonight?" We were both going to represent the company and she was my plus one. It was all business and nothing else. She was a daughter of a prominent family in Spain. She was good at her job and she was a great asset for the company. It also didn't hurt that she had vast connections in the country.

"Be ready by six. You can go home and get ready. I'm sure we'll be fine without you for the rest of the day," I said calmly, cocking my head quickly and going back to studying the paperwork I had in my hands. She leaned a little closer and grazed my cheek. Her perfume was heady and I wanted to get away.

"I'll be more than ready for you. See you tonight, mi amor," she purred and then sashayed her tight-clad body out the door.

Running my hand through my hair, I made a mental note to tell her I was seeing someone else. She seemed oblivious to the fact that I had declined her offers, several times. She simply kept on coming nonetheless. *Christ, that woman's going to be trouble.*

Releasing a heavy sigh, I went back to my office, sat on my desk and stared at the photo of the woman who had irrevocably bewitched me. It was a picture I had taken the day after making love to her. That night had been one of the best nights I'd ever had. She had definitely been worth the wait. When I'd woken up and seen her next to me, I had to keep a memento; to freeze that moment in my mind. She was everything that I'd ever wanted in a woman and more. I had grabbed my phone and taken the picture. Her hair was disheveled, lips slightly parted and the sheet barely covered her breasts. She looked so peaceful and absolutely breathtaking.

Something tugged inside of me the longer I stared at her. *Christ, Knightly, you've got it really bad.*

Pulling out my phone, I checked for messages or missed calls. I got a few from friends and work, but none had come from her.

I squeezed the bridge of my nose to ease some tension, and then buzzed the intercom, barking for Luke, my assistant who was hired a week ago in London, to come inside my office "this instant".

"Yes, Mr. Knightly?" the composed, blue-eyed, blonde male asked.

"Can you check my schedule? Tell me when I'm free so I can visit London."

After a minute or two, he came back again with the company iPad and checked the calendar. Clearing his throat, he spoke, "Next week, you can leave Friday afternoon, but you have to be back early Sunday to make it for your golf meeting with the Mayor and other investors."

"Fine, make sure the pilot knows. I want to leave at four and get there by six. Do it before you leave today. That will be it, Luke. Thank you."

"Good day, Mr. Knightly."

Fuck! Another week until I see her? Fuck!

Twenty-six
Sienna

"Owww," I yelped in pain when my tongue got burned by the scalding hot coffee. I'd been all over the place and my mind had decided to take a vacation somewhere in Marbella. The first thing I'd done this morning was check my phone for calls or messages. I was crushed when he never called or texted last night; he usually called me before he went to bed.

I huffed. If he was still mad at me, okay. I could deal with that, but what I couldn't fathom was someone telling me what to do. If he wanted to be with me, he had to change. I was not yielding to his demands.

I was on my way to Chad's studio in Camden town geared in an all-black ensemble; black cami, black pants and black pumps. It definitely matched my mood and I was in terrible need for girly time. I knew Chad was a man—technically speaking—however he was a woman at heart. His usual laissez-faire attitude would help pick up my mood.

Pulling open the door to his studio, I let myself in and called out his name. The main floor was his actual art studio where he did some of his shoots and his touch-and-go penchant for painting. He only painted when he was stressed out, though. His main focus, pride and joy was photography.

"In here, baby love!" Chad yelled behind the black drapes and I strolled over to him.

My shoes clicked loudly against the hardwood floors as I walked and my eyes scanned the room. The first thing I noticed was black. There were a lot of black drapes lining the room. The second thing I noticed was his equipment. There were a lot of scattered props; black chaise lounge, black covered bed, huge mirrors, metal working table with a lot of strategically placed work-man tools and an all-black Harley Davidson Hot Rod sat in the middle of the room.

I dauntingly stared at the bike. *Am I going to be on that thing? Or the guy named Troy?*

"Like it? It's such a sexy bike. I pulled some strings to get a loaner. It's going to be fabulous! Troy's here somewhere." Chad looked around and called out to him.

A man emerged from another black curtain draping on the other side of the room. He was dressed in a low-rise, all black Armani micro-modal trunk. Holy Shit! My eyes landed on his bulging mid-section and then grazed over muscled thighs and up towards his torso. *Whoa, was that an eight pack? I've never seen one up close.* He had the bad boy, dark hair going on. It was a little long, brushing over his jaw, unruly, but it gave him more appeal and a little edge. Dark hair, chocolate eyes and a sexy grin as he saw me check him out from head to toe.

Chad cleared his throat as I looked away embarrassed. *Crap.* "Troy Scott, meet Sienna Richards. Sienna, this is Troy," Chad introduced us jovially.

"Hello, Sienna. Finally! I get to meet you. Chad's been talking about you non-stop," the hot hunk said with a dark, deep voice in his British accent.

"Great to meet you, too! I hope Chad spoke kindly of me. He can get carried away sometimes," I said with enthusiasm. *He's hot, all right! However my man is even sexier and hotter by tenfold.*

So, stop staring at his body, hmmm?

"Enough with the pleasantries and let's get down to business, shall we?" Chad's business voice echoed in the room. *Okay, here goes.*

Chad directed me behind the drapes where Troy had come out of and gave me a silk-ruffled bikini panty, a small, black silk robe and four-inch, black suede boots that sat two inches above my knees—fuck-me boots he said—to change into. He immediately applied heavy, black eyeliner, false eyelashes and cherry red lipstick.

Troy was leaning against a table when I came out. I didn't even look at him because I was a little apprehensive about my lack of clothing. He was a model; I was sure these things didn't bother him, though to a novice like me, it was nerve-racking.

"Okay, Sienna, I want to get a few shots with you first. Can you stand in front of the mirror, cup your tits and take off your robe, please?" Chad already had his camera hanging around his neck and he had several strobes, umbrellas and reflectors all ready.

Holy, Shit! *Calm your nerves, Sienna. Just have fun and don't think.*

Music played in the background; "Teardrop" by Massive Attack. The beat certainly made it more sensuous. I walked over to the huge mirrors against the wall and my reflection stared back at me. *Yup! I look like an over-sexed, confident woman. Just pretend you are for today. Own it. I can do that, right?*

Chad asked me to turn around as I slowly slipped off my robe. He toyed with my long hair and asked me to open my legs a little wider while cupping my breasts. *Click. Click. Click.* "Stare back in the mirror and stick your tongue out over your upper lip. You look hot, Sienna." *Click. Click.*

His next shot had me lying on my stomach with my legs crisscrossed. "Lift your butt a little higher." *Click. Click.* "Beautiful. Now look at me. I want you to look into the camera with 'I want you' eyes." *Click.* "That's perfect love." *Click.* "Bite your bottom lip and look at me through your lashes. Think lustful thoughts. Give me that provocative face. Perfect!" *Click. Click. Click.* "Tilt your head to the right." *Click. Click.*

"Troy, you're on! Get on Sienna's back!" *Oh. My. God. Breathe, woman!*

I heard him approach. *Dear, me.* "Sienna, lift your butt again and pull your hair to one side. Troy, please get on top of her. Put one hand on her waist, the other on the bed to hold yourself and smell her neck."

Troy simply said "okay" like it was no big deal. I was sure it wasn't to him.

The bed dipped and I suddenly felt the warmth of his muscled body over mine. His covered penis was pressed on my ass as he gently placed his face near my neck. *Dear God! I feel hot all-over.* "Sexual perfection," Chad said.

Click. Click. Troy's breath was hot on my neck and it took a lot of power in me not to shiver.

"'Kay, now nibble her ear lobe." *Um, hell! This is torture.* The minute his tongue captured my lobe, I let out a soft moan. *FUCK!* "Beautiful, guys! Open your mouth a little wider, Sienna. Troy, hold her waist tighter like you can't wait to have her. You're seducing her into submission and will fuck her mindless!" *Click. Click. Click.* "Change positions. Get on the chaise lounge. Troy, sit comfortably, and Sienna, go straddle him while you take off the boots, please." *I guess I will just have to get over Troy being up close and personal with my boobs then.*

I walked over to where Troy sat, hoping that he'd be chipper so that it wouldn't have to be so awkward, but nope, he was unsmiling as I stopped opposite of him. Tucking my legs slowly on his hips and straddling him, he gave a deep groan. I didn't dare peek at him.

"Troy, kiss her neck and push your chest to her tits. Sienna, look straight at the camera and grab his shoulder." *Wow, this is intense. I'm going to strangle, Chad. Fuck! Blake won't be happy about this.*

Click. Click. Chad went behind me and took a few more pictures. "Sienna, I want you to lift your butt a little and then plump down on Troy, will you? Wrap your hands on his neck and look at me, love. Make the other men jealous." *Click. Click.* "Perfect. Troy, grab her ass with both hands." *Click. Click. Click.* He took a few more in different angles before he ended the session.

"Thank you, Troy, Sienna. I'll see you both Sunday at four?"

"Yeah, sounds good," Troy replied as he smiled at me. *Now he smiles, after the shoot.*

I wanted to cover my boobs, but it was pointless. He had an up close and personal introduction to my lady lumps. I gave him a non-committal smile and he escaped to go change as Chad handed me the black robe. I immediately slipped it on my barely-clad body.

"Thank you, baby love! I knew it was a bit hard for you to do this, however you were fantastic! Behind the lens, you looked like you've done it for years. If I were straight, I'd already have a hard-on just by looking at you."

I laughed. "It was a bit hard, but I'm doing this for you. You owe me big time!"

"Yeah, yeah. Now, go change so we can have dinner." I waited until Troy came out before I went to change back into my own clothing and I didn't even bother to take the make-up off. It fit perfectly with my all black get-up.

Chad and Troy were chatting like they were old buddies. I ignored them as I fished for my phone inside my purse, but no messages from Blake. *Does he plan to ignore me forever?*

Chad invited Troy to join us for dinner, but he declined because he had an early shoot tomorrow.

"Bye, Sienna. You were great!" Troy said.

I reddened. "Thank you! You were, too!" I mumbled. *I can't talk about it without getting shy and agitated. Ha!*

I followed Chad to his loft upstairs. He was making chicken pesto as I pulled out a bottle of white wine. "Chad, what's up with the soft porn shoot?" Glaring as I poured us both wine.

He chuckled and shook his head. "Baby love, it was hot! Troy was so turned on and you were, too." Cocking up a brow, he confirmed. "We all heard the moan." *No, shit.*

"Uh, duh? The man was sucking and nipping on my ear! Any woman would've reacted the same way. Throw a nun in there and she'd have the same reaction!" I tried to justify myself.

Sipping half of his glass in one gulp, he said, "I guess it helped a lot that he's got a marvelous body to boot, ey?" Chad sighed dreamily, thoughts wandering about Troy, I was sure. *He's hopeless.*

"Well, I suppose his body's pretty great! He does have that bad boy thing going on." *...and not to mention his nice ass?* I chuckled softly.

"Guess it's not that big of a deal since you've surrounded yourself with hot men lately, hmmm? There's Kyle, there's Troy and our god of sexiness, Blake. Must be nice, baby love!" He motioned for me to give him the pepper grinder and I placed it next to him.

"Kyle's a part of my past and we're working on our friendship. I hope working with him will help it recover, you know? As for Blake, he's still too intense for me, but I want him."

While he was making the sauce, he asked me about Blake. I told him the story starting from the moment we'd gotten back to his apartment that Saturday night. "I knew it! Blake's face said it all. Can you believe it? Blake is your boyfriend! How can you get all the luck, Sienna? I feel faint every time I see him smile. How do you stand it? He's such a marvelous piece of eye candy! I wish he had an identical gay twin!" He pouted as he fanned his cheeks. It was true; we both drooled over Blake! Who wouldn't? He was just über fucking yummy! I went over to hug him and promised that I'd dish out all the delicious details to keep him at bay. He bounced like a five-year-old.

I sat back in the chair, feeling a bit down. "It's great and all, but he hasn't contacted me for a whole day now. I'm worried. What if he found someone else? He wouldn't have to look too hard."

"Do you blame him? He has the right to be jealous. Kyle wants you back and he feels threatened. After all, Kyle's your first. He wouldn't dump you like that, though, love. It's Blake we're talking about. You're precious to him, even as a friend. Now that you guys are dating, you mean more to him. If it worries you that much, why don't you call him? He's probably waiting for you."

"I could call him tonight, I guess," I conceded.

"Splendid! Now, that's settled. Tell me, did he tell you he loves you yet?" His question caught me off guard so the wine went the wrong way and I was coughing mildly. *Uh, what the fuck?*

"Shut it, Chad! It's too early to be talking about love. This is about having fun and enjoying my youth! It was merely lust, not love; big difference there, Sherlock." *Was I in love with Blake? That's a little extreme. We barely just started. Love is not on the agenda.*

"Open your eyes, young lady! Have you seen how Kyle and Blake look at you? Their faces mirror each other. Fine, let's agree that Blake might not be there yet, but he's sure as hell making the trip to 'I Love Sienna Island' a little quicker. Trust me; I studied the guy's reaction that night, baby love. They're going to fight over you. Kyle was *the* love of your life. Blake is the present *lover* in your life." Chad looked at me thoughtfully. "The million dollar question is, if push comes to shove, who would you choose?"

I didn't answer him as he continued to make the pasta because I didn't have a response. I went to the living room and stared out the window. Kyle didn't know about Blake, yet. Once he found out, I knew he'd be devastated. *Will he fight for me? If he does, am I willing to hurt him?*

I shuddered.

I loved Kyle. I always had. I mean, who wouldn't? He had been my life before. *Do I love Blake? No, not that way. Although, my body has its own mind when he's around.* With Blake, I felt something... different. He evoked something profound within me. That was the intense part that I got scared about. He was too much and Kyle was familiar.

~S~

It was past eight-thirty when I got back to my apartment and I was extremely exhausted, but I wouldn't go to bed until I'd spoken to Blake.

The photo shoot had been interesting, to say the least. I rehashed everything in my head as I showered and brushed my teeth. *I'm sure when Sunday comes around, it won't be so awkward.*

Dressed in my pastel pink, silk slip, I sat on my bed and dialed Blake. After a few rings, he picked up. *Thank you, Jesus!*

"Sienna," Blake breathed out my name. Hearing his voice made my insides twist.

"Blake, you haven't been texting or calling. Are you still mad?" My voice was low and calm. My fingers toyed with strands of my hair. *Don't be; I'm going crazy here.*

"I was giving you time to cool-off, poppet. Have you missed me?"

Smiling like an idiot, I gushed, "I miss you. I miss you terribly. Are you still planning to visit this weekend?"

"I can't come out this weekend, poppet. I'm sorry. My schedule's chaotic. Hopefully next week, if I can manage."

I let out a disappointed sigh. "All right, promise to let me know when you are sure it's definite?"

"I promise, poppet." I could hear him smiling. I could picture him with that beautiful smile as he spoke on his cell.

He ended up talking about the galas and other parties he had attended for work. He asked me about the photo shoot with Chad. I gave him a cutout, subtle version and convinced him that he had to wait for the exhibition. After an hour of talking, we decided to call it a night.

I twisted and turned on my bed, while sleep eluded me. Thoughts of Blake—his voice, his smell—lingered through my mind.

My body ached for him.

My hand slowly went south as I relieved myself, thinking about the man who had hounded my thoughts endlessly from the moment he'd kissed me.

Twenty-seven

Since I didn't have classes on Friday, I slept in longer. Somewhere in my foggy mind I thought I heard Lucy buzz someone in. *I guess she's having friends over.*

My mind started to drift back to slumberland when someone knocked.

"Yeah?" I croakily called out, still not moving from my position.

"Morning, love! Sorry to be a bugger, but you have a delivery; a few of them, actually."

A delivery? I haven't ordered anything online lately.

I dragged myself out of bed to check where they had come from. There were three enormous, lime-colored, crystal vases with two dozen of my favorite oriental lilies in each one. I took the card that was attached to the first and opened it: *I want you.* My face glowed and beamed. I took the second card: *I miss you.* The third one said: *I worship you.*

I'm definitely charmed.

There was another knock on the door and Lucy opened it straight away. The deliverymen stood there with a gigantic box of pastries that had the world-renowned Pierre Hermé label. Two of the men went past us, heading directly to the living room with the box in their hands. I didn't see the man standing in the back of the others, so I jumped out of my skin when he greeted us.

"I apologize. I didn't mean to frighten you, but I'm looking for Ms. Sienna Richards?" a tall, lithe blonde with clear blue eyes asked Lucy and I. *Um, who is this man, again?* He'd never said.

"Um, that would be me. Who are you? Sorry, you didn't introduce yourself." I gave him a confused looked.

"I'm Luke Scott. I work for Knightly Industries as Blake Knightly IV's assistant. I was ordered by Mr. Knightly to come here." *Interesting.*

The deliverymen started to dissipate, exiting one by one, however Luke Scott stayed. He was smiling with a twinkle in his eye. Hmm...

"I think the room is ready. Let's all go and see."

Luce and I shared a what-the-fuck-is-going-on look as we followed Blake's assistant to the living room.

The coffee table had been transformed into a French pastry wonderland. Different flavors of authentic macarons were neatly organized in a towering pastry stand. Another tower was made of cream puffs, éclairs, napoleon, small Parisian cakes, fruit gateau, and pan au chocolat, to name a few. There were three silver platters of assorted chocolates and a bucket of champagne chilling in a silver bucket next to the coffee table and a coffee pot.

My eyes greedily roamed the contents as my stomach growled. *Right on cue, Blake.*

"Enjoy, ladies. Also, Ms. Richards, I was ordered to give you this." He took a small, soft-leather box out of his breast pocket.

"Uh, thanks. Um, why don't you join us, Luke?"

"The company jet is waiting for me in Gatwick actually. I have to get back to Marbella as soon as possible. There was a lot of traffic in Paris so I'm running late. There's an important meeting set for three this afternoon and it's already quarter to twelve, but thank you, Ms. Richards. I'll let my boss know how delighted you are. I didn't realize how romantic he could be," he said with a wink.

"Wait, did you just say you flew to Paris? *To buy pastries?*"

Goodness gracious.

"Yes, that was what Mr. Knightly ordered. I really must get going. Have a good day, ladies." He promptly left without much ado, leaving Luce and I staring at each other.

A shrieking laugh came from Lucy, who was obviously as excited as I was. "Sienna, what the hell have you done to poor Blake? He's obviously smitten. I knew it! It took longer than expected, but Toby predicted that Blake had his eyes set on you. I'm happy that he's making you happy."

"You could say that, I guess. It's just in the early days, but I do like him a lot." Okay, I was a bit embarrassed that I hadn't told her myself first.

"No wonder women clamor for him. Look at this! He had his assistant jetting off to Paris to fetch a few boxes of freshly baked pastries for his beloved. Oh, Sienna! It shows how much you mean to him when he goes to such lengths. Isn't that romantic?" she said dreamily.

It's more than romantic. It's downright disarming me. If this is his intent, then he's doing a stupendous job!

Luce and I sat as we poured each other drinks, champagne for her and coffee for me. We savored each pastry and compared which one was the best. It was an orgasmic dessert heaven.

"How I wish Toby would do something like this for me. I mean, not on the same scale of grandeur—the man doesn't own private jets—yet just as sweet and romantic." *Did I hear a tinge of sadness? I might just be imagining things.* They're crazy for each other.

I took a sip of my coffee, eyeing her warily. "Toby loves you and he has his own way of showing it. Everything okay with you guys?"

She let out a sigh and limply sat back with angst written all over her face. "It's been rather off for the last week. Something's wrong, but he's not telling me. I'll give him a few more days to tell, if not, then I'll have to find another way." *Uh oh.*

"Whatever it is I'm sure he has a good reason. He could be swamped with work, you know," I tried to ease her worries.

She shrugged and got up. "We'll see. Anyhow, I have to go meet a few of my schoolmates for a project. I'll help you clean up when I get back, okay? Tell Blake I enjoyed his impromptu." She went over to kiss my cheek, but I hugged her instead and gave her a little squeeze.

"It'll be okay," I whispered in her ear as she nodded and headed out the door. It was apparent that she was bothered about it. I hoped she would be okay.

The soft-leather box sat closed next to the tower of macarons. I was dying to know what was inside.

I jerked it open.

It was a bracelet. A lightweight, gold chain design with an oblong, gold medallion and a big, diamond-studded heart that had tiny diamond-studded B.K. initials on the bottom right. *Huh! Why would he put his initials there? Is this his way of laying it on Kyle when I start work tonight?*

I placed the bracelet back on the table, scrambled to get my phone in the bedroom and dialed Blake. When he picked up, I didn't even let him say hello. I was ready to chew him out.

"Knightly, you'd better explain to me and you'd better explain well! Tell me why you would give a present with *your initials* blatantly standing out? This present didn't just land here on the *very same day* I start working with Kyle for absolutely no reason, did it?" I was seething. If it were possible to have steam coming out of my ears, the room would have been muggy.

"Poppet, calm down. I wanted you to wear something that's from me. I commissioned it a day before you told me about your job. Is it possible that I wanted Kyle to stay back? Yes, I do. Do you ever plan on telling him?" his placid tone irked me somehow.

"I'll tell him, but not yet. It's too early for him. He barely just got here. I'm not going to risk the possibility of him spiraling out of control again." Why was he pushing the issue? I would tell Kyle in a month or so... *I think.*

"It's too early for him or *for you,* Sienna?" I stopped breathing from his tone of voice; he was controlling his own anger, though only barely. There was some noise in the background. "Mi amor, we have to go soon or we'll be late!" the accented voice of a woman spoke in the background. I felt like I had been punched in the gut.

"WHO THE FUCK IS THAT?" I yelled when I heard him speak to the woman, but I couldn't make out what was being said. My eyes started to water. *Was he cheating on me?*

"Oh, so now you pay rapt attention to me. I see how this is going, Sienna."

"Blake, are you seeing someone else? You have to tell me!" My voice cracked in pain.

"Why? So you can go back to Matthews again? Do as you wish, Sienna. I have to be somewhere important. I'll speak to you later." He hung up without even saying goodbye.

Less than an hour ago, I had been basking in Blake's sweet sentiments. How the heck had it unfolded like this? Okay, maybe I had over-reacted a little bit there. I shrugged it off. There was no point dwelling and crying. I had to meet Kyle in three hours and start work. I'd just have to busy myself and not think of Blake for now. I would deal with my emotions tonight.

In a little over an hour, I was ready to go and I still had an hour and half to kill. I went to my drawer and pulled the card and key Marie had given me out. I'd just surprise Kyle with my punctuality.

Since we were checking out rock bands tonight, I had to look the part... well sort of. I let my hair down, put on heavy eyeliner winged at both corners, lots of mascara and rose pink lipstick. I chose a hot pink, Hervé Léger bandage top, leaving my back purely bare, and black-fitted jeans that accentuated my butt nicely with hot-pink suede pumps.

I made a last jaunt to the full-length mirror to assess everything and, suffice to say, I looked pretty hot.

Suck it, Blake!

Placing all the essentials in my black clutch, I headed out the door.

Twenty-eight

I let out a slow whistle when the cab dropped me off at the address I'd given him. When Marie said "company apartment" I thought of an actual apartment, not a gated Victorian home.

I took out the card Marie gave me and punched in the code on the keypad attached to the wall. I heard a little metal screech and the gate opened slowly. *Was Kyle even home?* I had acted out of impulse and had totally forgotten to call to see if he was there or not.

When I got a little closer to the door, I heard loud music streaming from the window upstairs. Jeff Buckley, yep, he was home.

Fishing out the spare key, I opened the door. The home was decorated in black, white and silver splendor and the effect was gorgeous—a little cold—but still chic and gorgeous. I found the stairs on the left side corner and went to go hunt down Kyle. The music came from the room at the end of the hall that I assumed was the master bedroom.

I stopped outside the black door and knocked, but no one answered. Clearing my throat loudly, I let myself in. The room was decorated in baroque contemporary with accents of sapphire-colored designs. My eyes landed on the table next to where Kyle slept. My breath caught when I picked up a nine by twelve picture of us. The picture was taken a year ago. We were at Zuma beach watching the sunset. I sat in between his legs and took a bunch of shots. I was looking straight into the camera as he kissed me, smiling. What bothered me was the fact that I was glowing with such happiness; it was the look of love. I placed it back slowly as I jumped from my name being called out.

"Sienna?"

I turned around and was shocked. Kyle had beads of water dripping down his body with only a black towel draping his lower half.

Oh! Fuck. Me.

Shit! Why, oh why did I put myself in this position? My heart thudded like mad as the memories of that night in Santa Monica flashed through my mind. I stood there, frozen, and couldn't utter a damn word.

"Can I just say that, that top does your back incredible justice? You look so hot! I have my work cut-out for me tonight if the musicians start clawing you, baby." He strolled to where I stood and his freshly showered smell engulfed my senses.

"I had time to kill so I decided to stop by and use the key your mom gave me. I hope that's okay?" I mumbled, distractedly.

"Baby, you're not serious! Of course, it's okay; we're practically family." *What did he mean by that? Was it because we grew up together or because we agreed to get married at the age of twenty-seven?* "I've never seen you with this much eyeliner, but it looks good on you; very edgy and downright sexy as hell."

"Would it be too much to ask if you could put some clothes on?" I asked as I stared at his bright hazel eyes.

"Too many memories for you, baby?" I shook my head. "We both know you're lying, though I'm going to let that slide."

"Thanks. What's with the picture frame? Why did you bring it here?" His eyes darkened as he leaned closer, his mouth against my ear. His chest was pushed against mine.

"Because we were happy. Because we were so in love and the thought of losing you left a big hole in my heart. I needed a constant reminder—something to believe in—that we're going to get back together. We were extremely happy and perfect for each other. It'll dawn on you someday that you are meant to be with me... and, when that time comes, I'll be here... waiting for you." His eyes had a little moisture in them. *Oh, Kyle. Please don't do this. Not tonight.* I wiped the corners of his eyes and he smiled widely. "Did I tell you how much I love you today?" *Am I forever doomed to be pulled back and forth?*

"Kyle, you know how I feel about this. I already told you, please, seeing you like this... tears me inside. It was so much easier when you had Brooke. I didn't have to dwell on it much."

"I know, baby. No worries, as I said, I love you and I'll wait. However long it takes until you want me back."

Jesus, this has got to stop. "What if that never happens? What then?"

"I know what I want. I'll take my chances."

"Whatever."

He gave me a quick kiss and left to go change.

~S~

The venue was on Chalk Farm Road and Kyle ushered me in with a tight grip on my waist to an empty booth. As soon as we sat down, he excused himself to go to the bar to order some drinks. I guess part of the job was drinking, having fun and skillful negotiating abilities.

I hoped his binge drinking days wouldn't affect him being around alcohol and drugs. The music industry was famous for that.

After that dreadful scene in his bedroom, he acted like nothing happened and I silently thanked him. We ended up ordering pizza and discussed the band that was playing tonight. The Cold Conflict was the band's name. We listened to their recorded songs earlier and I was impressed. They sounded like Lifehouse and Jeff Buckley put together and I was actually super excited to see them play tonight. *How great is this job?* Kyle was going to talk to them after their set and hopefully sign them on at the end of the night.

The place was starting to get packed when we arrived. I guess the band was going on very soon. I checked my phone and was surprised I had five missed calls from Blake. *Call him back or ignore? Do I really want to spend the next few hours wondering?*

Pressing the call button, the other end started to ring. The place was starting to get noisy so I had to duck a little bit lower. I didn't want to go outside since I was technically working and I didn't want to take advantage of the fact that Kyle probably wouldn't mind if I did take the call outside.

"Sienna, thank you for calling me back! I got worried when you didn't pick up my calls." The relief was evident in his voice and my stomach got the usual flip-flop from hearing it.

"Yeah, um... do you mind if we talk later? It's getting really noisy in here."

Of course, Kyle's timing was perfect as he slid into the booth and glued himself next to me. "Who are you talking to, baby?" he yelled against my ear, loud enough for Blake to hear. The violent growl I heard at the other end of the phone made me flinch.

Fuck-fuckity-fuck.

"Baby, who's that?"

I gave Kyle a death stare. "I'm talking to Blake."

"Tell him I said hi. TCC will be on shortly; you should call him back later when we're done," he shouted over the growing noise.

"*Sienna, if you hang up* IT'S OVER!" Blake said with a snarl, but it cracked at the end.

Is he going to be this jealous all the time? We've been fighting non-stop.

"Listen, Blake, I'll speak to you later, okay? The band's about to start. Bye." I ended the call without hearing his reply because I might have cracked from the pain it would have caused me.

TCC started to set-up. They were tuning and adjusting their instruments. The front man introduced himself as Will and thanked everyone for coming out tonight before they started playing. After a couple of songs, my phone vibrated.

Message received from Blake Knightly, it said.

I opened the text and a picture downloaded. It was a picture of a beautiful woman. She had ebony hair and arched brows, creamy skin and striking blue eyes with a complimenting, seductive smile. Her pose was purely inviting to the person taking the picture; Blake. She had a red silk gown on that flaunted her boobs. The formal outdoor setting in the background suggested that they were at an event.

Who is this woman? Did she work for him? My hands shook violently as I read the message attached at the bottom.

Blake: *I guess we can both have fun tonight. How about it, Sienna? She already said yes. She's always willing and eager to be serviced by the boss.*

No, no, no, no, no. My head spun. I felt sick.

I excused myself from Kyle who was giving his undivided attention to the band. He asked where I was going and I pointed at the restroom sign.

The bathroom was empty. I stood in front of the mirror for ten minutes just staring at my reflection. My mouth wobbled, yet I did not and would not cry. The message tore me to pieces, but I had the rest of the night to hold it together. If he wanted to fuck another woman, then I couldn't stop him.

Good riddance, over-indulgent playboy!

A hysterical laugh bubbled out of me. Funny how it was just this morning he said he worshipped me in that damn card? I clasped my hands on the sink, my head bowed. I chanted in my head:

Breathe. Clear your head. Focus.
Breathe. Clear your head. Focus.
Breathe. Clear your head. Focus.

After twenty minutes in the bathroom, I decided to go back to the table before Kyle started looking for me. When he saw me, he gave me a thumbs-up and I smiled at him. The first set ended and Kyle gestured that he'd go meet the band and bring them around to the table.

I smiled at the platinum Patron sitting on the table. Bless the man who still knew my drink! I poured myself a double shot and cringed lovingly when I sucked the lemon slice.

Work face, on, I commanded myself to function. *Smile. They're heading over.*

It was a difficult thing to do, especially when my heart was breaking, however this was work. Not only would it be unprofessional of me to break down and cry, it would also reflect badly on Kyle.

Yeah, it was horrible, but this was life.

Twenty-nine

The band consisted of five rowdy men. They introduced themselves as Spike, Roger, Brandon, AJ and Will. Will immediately slid next to me and AJ on the other side, the rest filled in, leaving Kyle sitting on the right end.

The guys were fun to be around and, in the span of five minutes, we were all sharing jokes and laughing out loud. Everyone helped themselves to the drinks on the table. After Kyle noticed they were settling in, he shifted the conversation to business. He broke down the benefits of signing with them and the advantages and opportunities M.A.T.T. Music could provide. The guys each had their own sets of questions and Kyle responded to each one with great detail. Kyle was pretty amazing in action. I didn't know why it never occurred to me to follow him around when he worked back in LA.

"So Sienna, where do you come into the picture?" Will suggestively asked.

"I'll be helping with correspondence between your lawyers and managers and confirming bookings for gigs and shows... the usual lot."

"I like that! I like knowing that we have you on the team," he said, winking at me.

What's with men and their constant flirting, seriously?

"Hey! We're up for the second set in five," AJ, who had thick eyeliner on, announced to the group. They grumbled and slid off the booth.

"Save a dance for me later?" Will asked in a hushed tone.

"Sure," I murmured.

Will winked at me before he took over the microphone.

"Did he just wink at you?" Kyle's disbelieving face made me laugh.

"I don't advise mixing business with pleasure, Sienna." *Yes, sir!*

"I won't. No need to worry about that."

My purse taunted me, but I wasn't going to check it, just in case there were more pictures waiting to be opened.

I poured myself a couple more shots before TCC ended their second-set. Everyone applauded and hollered at them. They were pretty great.

The music changed into upbeat dance music and people started to fill the tiny space that was the dance floor. Will came over immediately after exiting the stage and we both agreed we'd take a shot before dancing.

Dancing with him was lively and entertaining. I was having so much fun that we ended up dancing to three songs. When we got back to the table, the men agreed to sign, but needed their manager to speak to Kyle about money. Kyle was ecstatic and promised to call their manager the next morning and hopefully, by Monday, the contract would be drafted, if all went according to plan.

With business out of the way, everyone relaxed. Kyle excused both of us with the reason of "work" and needing to talk outside.

My lungs happily welcomed the fresh air. I was tipsy and buzzing quite nicely, just what I needed.

Kyle pulled me to the other side of the building that had fewer people chatting and hanging about. "You okay, baby?" He caressed my cheek softly.

"Yep, I'm stupendous!" He pulled my body closer to him and his warmth felt comforting.

You've really lost your marbles. I closed my eyes, feeling the hot, coursing effect of the alcohol in my body.

Blake. Blake. Blake.

My mind was fighting the images of Blake and the woman flashing in my head.

Kyle captured my mouth softly. His kiss was gentle and not fevered or demanding like Blake's. I sighed softly as Kyle's smell penetrated my nostrils. It reminded me of high school, the beach and yesteryears.

He closed in on me and pushed me gently against the wall. He cupped my breast and squeezed it. That instantly made me snap my eyes open. *Don't do this to yourself. Walk away before it gets messier.*

Think. Brain. Think.

I placed a hand on Kyle's chest. "I can't do this with you right now. I'm sorry. We'll talk about it soon, but not tonight."

"Does it have anything to do with Blake?" he hissed. He was grinding his teeth so loudly it made me cringe.

"Possibly. I'll call you, okay? I'm going to go home. I don't feel too well."

I kissed him on the cheek before he pulled me to him, gave me a tight hug and told me again how much he loved me. He wanted to get me a cab, but I convinced him I needed a minute or two to clear my head. He finally agreed and went back inside where TCC was waiting for him to party with them.

Leaning against the building, I closed my eyes. *How about I just go home and wallow? Maybe I can drink myself to sleep then I wouldn't have to think at all.*

"Sienna, is that you? It *is* you; what's wrong? Did that man do something to get you upset?" My eyes flickered to life, looking for the owner of that voice. It didn't sound familiar to me.

"It's Troy, from Chad's photo shoot Thursday." Oh, yeah.

"Hey! Fancy seeing you here! And no that man didn't get me upset, there's just so much going on with life, that's all." I looked down and studied my black lacquered nails.

"Let's get you some good food then you can spill your problems, deal?"

Boy, that made me smile. "You're crazy! Go back to your friends, Troy."

"I'm not leaving you when you're sad. Let's walk to the place. It's only a couple of blocks and you can make a decision then, if you want to go in or not. How's that sound?"

"Okay, deal." *He doesn't even know me and yet he's willing to listen to my problems? That's odd and unexpectedly very sweet of him.*

We were both consumed with our own thoughts as we walked. He stopped outside a pub, hands in his pockets. "What's it going to be, Sienna?

"What the hell. I don't want go home this early anyway."

We ordered hamburger sliders, fish and chips, beer for him and a margarita for me. I didn't realize how hungry I was until after the food was set on the table. We talked, ate a bit, drank some and talked some more.

I learned that he was recently divorced; six months ago. His wife cheated and he caught them in action in their marital home. *He's probably still hurting too. Being cheated on can be traumatizing; not to mention the big dent something like that puts in your ego and self-esteem.*

Since he spilled his own secrets, I spilled mine. I gave him the cutout edition of Kyle cheating, Blake sweeping in, Kyle moving, Blake going ballistic and the beat went on.

"Do what makes you happy, Sienna. No one knows what that is except you."

"I know." I smiled, nudging him lightly on the arm.

Before I knew it, the time was hitting half past one. He insisted on taking me home since I had drunk three more margaritas.

We took a cab back to my flat. He asked the driver to wait for a few minutes. He insisted that he see me to my apartment door, not the building entrance. We rode the elevator silently and I checked him out for the first time that night. He was wearing a leather jacket with jeans and he was very good-looking. Why did his wife have to screw around? He was one of the good guys.

Stepping out the elevator, we stopped outside my door as I fished for my keys. "Thank you for tonight. You really made my night. When you're feeling down and out, I'll take you out for beer, fish and chips and sliders to make you feel better." He chuckled softly.

I slid the key in the lock and opened the door. He handed me his phone.

"Program your digits, in case I take you up on that offer."

I stifled a laugh as I punched my information in. I put my name down as 'Sexiness is Sienna' and we both laughed when he saw what I did.

He kissed my cheek softly and left.

Thirty

My throat was dry and I was absolutely parched, the wonderful effects of alcohol. *Oh heck!* It was dark and I was too drunk to flick the switch.

Water. I need water. I staggered to the kitchen and poured myself a tall glass of agua. My phone vibrated. *Oh, hell.* I went to flick the light switch in the kitchen as I located my phone.

Kyle.

Grudgingly, I took the call. "Hello?"

"Did you get home safe? Why did it take you this long to pick up?"

Honestly, I was not in the mood to explain anything. "Sorry to make you worry, buster, but I just got home."

"What, just *right now?* Where the heck have you been?"

"Out with a friend. Listen, I'll call you tomorrow. Sleep. Going to sleep now. Peace," I mumbled.

Who explains when they're drunk, anyway? Hangover's going to be a bee-otch tomorrow.

I swallowed the rest of my water and slammed the glass down on the counter.

"Having the time of your life?" A deep voice came from somewhere in the blackened section of the living room.

I jumped, shrieking as the shadow came out of the darkened room.

Blake.

Oh, for the love of God! Did he have to come here wearing his tux? He looked like what dreams were made of... and that woman had probably enjoyed him quite thoroughly, too. The thought made me want to puke.

"For crying out loud, what is it with you brooding and scaring people out of their wits? How long have you been waiting?"

"I've been here for about three hours waiting for you to get home. Who was the man outside the door? He's British, certainly, not Matthews," said the observant man.

Where does he get the nerve to just barge in here after what he put me through before?

"None of your business," I said deadpanned and turned to flee, wanting the security of my room. Blake yanked me back by my arm and cornered me at the kitchen counter. *Oh my, he smells extra delicious tonight.* My drunken body was already betraying me. *Fuckin' A!*

"What the hell are you wearing? Do you see how bare your back *is*?"

"WHO CARES ANYMORE? Go back to where you came from and LEAVE ME ALONE," I screeched at him while trying to free my arm from his titanium-like hold.

"No."

"What do you mean 'no?' Go back to that wretched woman in the picture you sent me. Go fuck each other's brains out until you both can't walk anymore. *I. Don't. Care!*"

"What did you *do* with that man, Sienna?" I stared him down, not willing to answer his question. "Fucking answer me!"

I kept still. I wasn't going to. That picture and message he'd sent earlier wreaked havoc in my thoughts. Images of him kissing her and touching her body the way he did mine caused my stomach to free-fall.

I'm too drunk to be doing this.

I was so drained from all the drama that was disrupting my life my sanity teetered at the edge of a cliff.

When I tried to pull my hand away again, he let me go. I sprinted to my room and sat on the bed, slightly shaken. *Why did he have to show up here? To continue this farce after he slept with someone else?* My lips wobbled. I bit them—hard—until I tasted blood.

I felt him watching me from the doorway. He was at the foot of my bed in a few strides, lowering himself and sitting on his heels. He placed his hands on my knees.

I was speechless as I watched the man, shivering.

"*Please...*" Blake whispered. His voice heavy, anguished. With one word, all of my erected barriers fell apart.

My mind boggled with everything that happened. "Explain that message."

If it were another man, I would've just shut the door on his face. He never failed to get under my skin, past my defenses. He knocked them down until I was barefaced and unmasked.

"That was immature; I admit that. It was wrong of me to inflict the kind of pain you associate with your ex, but I couldn't stop the thoughts of you with him. When I heard his voice in the background; it pulled the trigger. I was livid, delirious, unhinged with anger. I slept with Amelia a few months ago—" My heart *literally* stopped beating. *Oh, no. Don't do this to me.* I tried to move, but he was like steel, holding me in place. I was stuck facing him. "I haven't touched another woman since you became mine. *I swear on my dead parents,* I would never—*ever*—do that to you. You make me so happy; I get paranoid thinking that I'll lose you to someone else. It's terrifying. Forgive my offenses, my weaknesses, my failings, my flaws. I only want to be with you."

I jerked his arm and lightly shook him. "Promise me, you won't hurt me that way again. I don't think I can get past it and forgive you if you do." He got up and sat next to me and pulled me in his lap, cradling my body.

"I give you my word. I promise it won't happen again. Today's been hell and I couldn't go through it anymore without seeing you. I left the event an hour after I got there and flew straight to you. I'm glad that I did. I'm sorry, poppet..." I placed my hands on the back of his skull and pulled his lips to mine.

The boiling, fevered kisses that I yearned for so many days turned into reality; and boy, were they better. I'd never hungered for any other man like this. His kiss lit me on fire. My body couldn't get enough of him. I shifted, straddling his hips and rubbing myself on him as our kisses became violent and uncontrollable.

Blake... show me... need me... love me... my thoughts spun as we groaned together. He ground my hips tightly against his. My body was freefalling into the abyss as his hands became urgent. I wrenched my hands from the back of his head and tugged the ends of my fitted bandage top.

"I want... more..." I didn't know what I meant by that, my emotions were all over the place. *Since when did I want more?*

We took off our clothes in haste until we were skin to skin. Every touch made me weaken. He circled my waist and lowered me on the sheets, his body covering mine. The room was dark, but the streaks of light through the windows showed enough for me to clearly see his body.

Our faces were inches apart as we stared at each other. By the way we were looking at one another, one could tell there was something going on. I couldn't speak. I was afraid of what would come out of my mouth and I didn't think I was ready to commit myself that quickly, but at the same time, I couldn't seem to control how I reacted to him.

I can't fall for him. It will end me. However I had; I loved him already, and I needed to stop denying it. My thoughts rammed into realization. *I love him and I didn't even know I was falling in love.*

His impassioned eyes zeroed in on mine.

Fuck! Don't let him see it. Please.

"Sienna..." Blake said in a husky voice. What bothered me was how he said my name; it was loaded with meaning.

He kissed me slowly and passionately. Gone was the man who wanted me with wild abandon. Gone was the man who handled me roughly like a savage animal that couldn't survive if he didn't get inside me any sooner. The man tonight was soft and gentle. His fevered kisses remained intense, but were soft, unguarded. He kissed my body with thorough tenderness and when his tongue touched my slick folds; his eyes never left my face as I came apart in his mouth. He took his time as he kissed my stomach and slowly made his way to my breasts, fondling, sucking, and biting.

With his body ensconced over mine, he kissed me with pure yearning and honesty. My mind shut down and I let my body speak to him as I linked my arms around his neck, my legs hooking behind his back, drawing his body closer.

He broke off the kiss. Our eyes fixated on each other. His drew me in and I couldn't look away as I felt his cock gently hover over my opening. He never looked away as he coaxed himself gently inside me. He watched me gasp as he filled me to my core, kissing me tenderly as he slipped in and out of me with unhurried focus.

He's making love to me. My eyes burned as I got choked up with emotion.

Blake... I love you... I whispered in my head.

I was kissing him lovingly, baring my soul to him. My hands held his ass cheeks, my nails digging into his skin. He went deeper and I moaned against his lips. His pace started to increase as I lifted my hips, meeting his thrusts. He pulled away from my kisses as his eyes bore into me, watching my frenzied response to him as he took my body to another level of ecstasy.

I was panting and running out of breath. I felt my stomach tightening and clenching, readying for an orgasm. His body started to tense as he began a swifter pace. His teeth found my neck and bit it. I yelled out his name as my orgasm rocked my body off its foundation. His heavy breathing was hot on my ear as his hands gripped my hips, grounding them into place, as his body demanded its own release. He said my name with a guttural growl deep in his throat as his body tensely. I felt his cock twitch and then the gush of his semen filled me. His lips found mine again and kissed me tenderly; my heart contracted. He pulled out of me and gathered me close to him. I was spent and exhausted from the intense lovemaking.

My breathing started to even out and my eyes fluttered closed. His heartbeat was beating wildly against my back as he tightened his hold on me, kissing the back of my neck. "I love you," he whispered against my ear.

I squeezed my eyes tighter. *I love you, too...*

His bare admission tore my insides. I evened out my breathing, pretending I was asleep.

~S~

I woke up with a start when I felt the cold air hit my back. I rolled to the other side, reaching for him. I hugged his body from behind. I nuzzled the back of his neck, inhaling his scent like a starved woman. *I love him...*

My hand trailed over his broad shoulders and down to his abdomen. The ridges of his six-pack, toned abs teased my fingers. My hand moved lower and found his semi-hard penis. *Damn, even asleep his cock is huge.* I stroked him gently as it started to come to life from my hasty ministrations.

I smiled. *Well, hello, bad boy.*

I gently turned him on his back as a soft sigh came from his lips, he was obviously still asleep. I smiled devilishly as I stared at his glorious body. *I want him... and I'll be damned if I have to wait for him... my aroused state can't wait for him any longer.*

I took him in my mouth, teasing him with my tongue and, at the same time, bringing it to the back of my throat with determined suction. He moaned. I sucked him until his cock was rigid with throbbing need. I moved my body so that I was over his hips and straddled him, guiding his cock with my hand and coaxing it slowly inside me. I moaned with satisfaction, *my God, he feels so good.* I recoiled slowly as my insides adjusted to his size. This position made the filling penetration mind-blowing and grippingly intense. I moved slowly at first, my stomach quivering from the intensified strokes of his penis inside me.

My palm sat on his chest to balance me as the other cupped my breast. The heightened carnal intensity drove me to ride him harder. I felt his hand pinch my nipples and I growled with delight.

"Take what's yours, my love," Blake ordered, husky and aroused after my ministrations, making me even more crazed and hungry.

I want it all.

Leaning back and placing my hands on his thighs, I rode his cock with fervent need. My mind shut down as my body convulsed around him. I yelped out his name softly as I recovered from my climax. He held me down as he ejaculated.

Lifting my head off his chest, I stared at his delighted face. "Fuck that was amazing. You're one hell of rider, poppet."

I laughed huskily as lay down next to him and nuzzled the crook of his neck. "You're welcome."

"I thought I had died and gone to Heaven when I woke up to you moaning with your eyes closed, enjoying my cock for your own greedy pleasure."

"I can't seem to get enough of you... I don't think I ever will," I admitted softly against his neck, my eyes heavy with exhaustion.

"As do I, my love, as do I," his sleepy voice murmured.

Thirty-one

It had been almost five weeks since I last saw Blake, but we kept each other updated with everything. I was soaring high because our relationship was growing steadily and I loved him a little bit more every single day. I hadn't told him how I felt. I wasn't ready for that yet. It would be hard to take it back once I told him and I didn't want it to be held against me.

The morning after Blake left for New York, I met up with Chad and Troy for the shoot. It lasted around five hours and even though I was only wearing skimpy underwear, Troy made me feel at ease as we laughed and joked around. Though there were times in the shoot where his eyes became stormy when I draped my body over his or when he groaned as my nipples touched his chest. He was hot, to be sure; who wouldn't be attracted to an extremely hot man like him? But I didn't let this bother me because I knew, deep down, there was only one man I wanted.

I eased Blake's doubt by wearing his bracelet and convincing him that I didn't want anyone else. Kyle warily eyed the bracelet, but never asked about it. He knew I was dating Blake and I was grateful that he never asked and didn't push the issue. Our friendship strengthened over the weeks and I felt like we were almost back to where we were before. Almost.

I hadn't seen Chad since the last shoot. He'd been busy preparing for his show. My time was consumed with school and working with Kyle. Luce and I barely caught up with our lives since school demanded a lot of her time with projects and applying for internships.

Today, Blake would be arriving from New York and I couldn't wait to see him. He was scheduled to arrive late in the afternoon so we'd see each other at Chad's exhibition on King's Road. I'd primed my body for this long awaited reunion and I couldn't wait to get him alone. I'd been scouring the shops for a perfect dress for the last week. I hoped I got the reaction I was aiming for.

My hair was in a high ponytail. I applied make-up carefully with light eye shadow and thick eyeliner winged on the both ends. I then swiped two coats of mascara on both my upper and lower lashes, making my eyes look a fiery, piercing golden green. I highlighted my cheeks with bronzer and finished it with candy pink colored lipstick, dabbing lip-gloss on my bottom lip and puckering to get the full effect.

I went over to my bed and took the nude, designer, bandage dress that fitted my body like a glove; leaving little to the imagination. It was short, maybe a few inches below my butt and the top part pushed my breasts up, giving me a hefty amount of cleavage. I slipped on my nude designer Rolando pumps and skimmed over my appearance in the full-length mirror. *I look good*, I thought as I admired how the dress showed off and complimented my figure. I wanted Blake's eyes to pop out of their sockets when he got a glimpse of me.

There was a soft knock at the door indicating Kyle's presence. Grabbing my clutch purse, I headed out to meet him.

"Coming," I called out as I closed the door behind me.

His face looked dumbstruck as he stared at me. I smirked as his eyes took me in. *Hopefully, I will get that same reaction from Blake.* "Goddamn, baby. You look like a piece of Heaven."

Rolling my eyes, I grabbed his hand and dragged him towards the elevator. "Let's get moving, lover boy; I don't want to be late or Chad will cook us for dinner."

We were five minutes away from King's Road as the cab weaved through the traffic. I fidgeted uneasily in my seat. *Which images did Chad choose?* He'll have fifty portraits up for display, but said he needed twelve from our shoot and the rest was filled with his other models. *What if they look stupid and awkward?*

I grunted my frustrations. Kyle reached out for my hand, clasped it with his and placed it on his lap. "Baby, it's going to be fine. You're worrying for nothing," he assured, smiling brightly as he kissed my hand. The cab stopped outside the gallery.

My heart was in my throat and I was anxious to see the images Chad chose.

We entered the building and a uniformed waiter with champagne flutes greeted us. I took two flutes and gulped them, one after the other, like they were water. *Okay, now I'm better.* Kyle shook his head in amusement.

I looked around me and saw Chad's perfect artistry at its best. *Wow, that friend of mine is hella gifted.* One of the images was of a woman at the repair shop as she posed provocatively, bare-naked. Another was of a man and a woman on the hood of the car making love in a cemetery. My eyes took in the portraits. An image of a woman holding a guitar looked captivating. Another image was of a woman with two men posing illicitly against each other, but it was done in a way that provoked sexual thoughts and yet, pulled off the look of making it chic. I passed by them, feeling all hot and bothered as people gathered in admiration.

It was sex, sex and more sex.

Sex blanketed the whole gallery as people buzzed about Chad's eye for beauty. As provocative as they were, he made the images look sophisticated somehow and not raunchy. He managed to capture that essence of the moment where you feel like you're there with them and you're watching them in the act. It was beautiful.

"Baby love, finally, you're here! What do you think?" Eyeing me, cautiously, gauging my reaction.

"Chad you're a genius! These are quite amazing! Tonight's your big break, baby! You had better not forget me when you go global." I hugged him tightly as my heart soared for him. I knew how long he'd been waiting for someone to acknowledge his work and after tonight, he'd be the toast of London.

"As if! There's no way a person can forget you, baby love. You have a way of making people remember you."

Do I? Huh.

Smiling, I hugged his waist. "Who's all here? Luce and Toby?"

"She texted me a few minutes ago. She said they'd be here in ten to fifteen minutes, tops."

The gallery was filling up with a lot of artsy people. *Where are the portraits of me and Troy?* I looked around for Kyle, but he was nowhere in sight.

"If you're looking for Kyle, he's at the encore of the show. Come, I'll show you." Holding my elbow with his hand, he guided me towards the end of the room and made a quick left. He showed me to another room, which was dimmer and darker. The only lighting came from the ceiling directly above each of the twelve portraits of Troy and me. My breath caught.

The images were impressively stunning. The woman in the picture was seductive, confident and in-charge of her world. I was rendered speechless.

Chad placed an arm around my shoulders. "Now do you see what everybody else sees, baby love? Never let the past dictate you. Don't berate yourself because you aren't tall enough or you don't have a slimmer figure. You're beautiful, *inside and out, scars and all.* I wanted these images to capture how I see you—how we all see you—so that you'll realize how special you are. You're a strong woman, love, no matter what life throws at you, you always come out braver than before. It's time to be free of the shackles because if you don't, the Browns win. *Look around you. This woman is bold and fearless.*"

I got choked up as I turned my body and hugged him with all of my heart. "Thank you," I whispered in a wobbly voice. He was such a good friend and I would always remember what he had done for me. I would never forget it.

"That's what friends are for. *Let's not ruin our make-up, hmmm?* Go over to Kyle." He pointed to the far right corner. "I have to greet my other guests in the other room."

I nodded and whispered "I love you" as he kissed my forehead and whispered the same words back to me.

I went over to where Kyle was standing and staring intently at my image. I was on the bed with underwear on and my boobs were covered with only a drape of a black silk sheet. One leg was on the bed with the other leg slightly bent above it. Both of my arms were above my head, lips parted, as I stared provocatively at the camera. *Oh, that looks hot!*

Kyle was silent as he took in the image. I didn't say a word because he had a pained expression. *Odd, not the impression I would've thought it would provoke.*

"That morning in Lake Tahoe, you looked exactly like this when I came out of the shower and I thought to myself, *how lucky am I? I have a gorgeous woman who loves me to bits.* I felt blessed. Seeing this portrait makes me see what I had lost again."

Fuck, I didn't expect him to say that. That was the morning after we had made love for the first time. I remembered seeing him coming out of the shower and my heart had happily swelled at the sight of him.

Fuck-fuckity-fuck.

This night was becoming an upheaval of emotions. Kyle's, I could do without. I felt shaky inside and I didn't know what to say to him, so I stayed quiet.

A squeal broke from another room. I smiled at Lucy's enthusiasm. I kindly excused myself to meet Lucy in the other room and he smiled sadly at me. *Fuck, Kyle. Don't do this to me*, my eyes pleaded.

I gulped some air after I left the room. I found Luce and Toby talking animatedly with Chad. I went over to join them and we all gushed over Chad. He looked so happy and my heart contracted seeing him like that. A few people came over to get him, wanting to introduce him to some other guests. All three of us went to check out some other portraits. I chuckled throatily as I found Lucy's face flushed from the images before her.

"Sienna Richards," a booming, deep voice behind me announced. I turned and found Troy smiling elatedly.

"Troy! How are you?" I squealed from surprise. I hadn't seen him for a month and I was excited. I gave him a tight hug.

"Are you trying to give me a cardiac arrest? 'Cause you're about to accomplish that if you come any closer with that miniscule dress on." I reddened. *Holy guacamole! Was he flirting with me? That's a first.*

"Cheeky tonight, aren't we?" I jested back at the handsome hunk of a man.

His gaze fell on Lucy and Toby who were watching the exchange with interest. "Hello, I'm Troy. Sienna's counterpart in the shoot." They all shook hands and Luce smiled brightly at the sight of him.

Troy looked like his usual hot self, scruffy and rugged with his well-worn jeans and black leather jacket. He had a tad bit of extra dangerous edge when he puts his hair in that tiny ponytail. *He's such a badass.* One time he arrived at Chad's on a Ducati 848, black on black motorcycle. I swooned then. *Hot* guy and a *hot* piece of motorcycle; totally too *HOT* to handle!

When Toby and Troy started talking about football, Luce whispered in my ear. "He's quite a hot hunk,

Sienna! He seems *too keen* on you. Just be careful. Blake might not be too happy about that. You know how he gets." *Yes, I do know, but he has nothing to worry about. I love him... but he doesn't know that... yet.*

"So, where are these infamous portraits of yours?" Toby asked and I pointed them to the other adjacent room. When they left, Troy moved closer with a smile that made his eyes dance. *Hmmm, what's he up to now?*

Amused, I had to ask, "What?"

Troy shook his head. "Your pictures were really great. Chad managed to capture your vulnerability and your sass at the same time. I actually asked him to print and send me all twelve portraits, in a smaller scale of course." *Get out of here! No way!*

"Why would you do that? You liked 'em that much?"

"You just sizzled and besides, we looked good together. The chemistry was palpable in those pictures," Troy said, looking me straight in the eye. My mouth ran dry. *No shit.* I remembered during the shoot, I would tremble from his extra close proximity. Or a moan would escape me when his breath reached my ear or when his chest grazed my nipples.

A waiter passed by and I turned around to get a flute of champagne. Sipping the champagne soothed my scattered nerves.

My back was turned to Troy. He came up behind me, almost touching, but not. I felt the heat of his body as his hot breath touched my ear. My eyes were glued to the champagne flute in my hand as his voice filtered through the music being played. "I want to see more of you. Think about it. You know my number." With that neck hair-raising encounter, Troy parted and joined his friends who gathered close to the entrance where there was a lounge area.

I blinked a few times. *What just happened? Did he just ask me out?*

No shit, Sherlock.

Draining my drink, I went to look for my friends when a dark figure across the room stopped me in my tracks. I went over to him, but my excitement halted when I saw his scowl. "You came!" I stammered.

"Yes, I was invited if it escaped your notice." I deserved his cold treatment, but it didn't help lessen the pain that gnawed at my heart.

I went closer, cradling the sides of his face and kissing his beautiful, sexy mouth for a good minute and released him. *Ouch, he barely opened his mouth.* "You have no idea how much I've missed you," I told the man who had me on tenterhooks as I took in how handsome he looked in a dark grey suit. He thawed a little bit, just a *wee* bit.

"Blake! Good to finally see you emerge from your tycoon lifestyle!"

"I wouldn't miss your debut, Chad. You should know better."

Touched by Blake's support for him, Chad held his hand close to his heart. "Thank you. You don't know how much your support means to me. Lover, would it be okay if I steal your girlfriend for a second? There's a bunch of people who want to meet her."

"Of course, as long as you don't let her out of your sight. Men are eyeing her like vultures ready to pounce." *Damn. Way to go, Blake.*

Blake asked where my portraits were and Chad pointed to the room as he guided me to a group of artsy people chatting. They were painters and photographers, some independent and some who worked with famous magazines and celebrity portraits. It was an impressive group and I enjoyed our conversation. They wanted to know if I would model for them. I kindly told them that I'd think about it. After spending a good fifteen minutes with them, I excused myself to find Blake. I passed Lucy and Toby who were talking to another couple. Toby smiled, but Luce stopped me. "What's up?" I asked her.

"Blake and Kyle are having words. You should rush before they rip each other's heads off."

I was about to turn left when an angry looking Kyle sprinted by, almost knocking me over. "Baby, you okay? I didn't see you. I'm sorry." I held his arm as I looked at him questioningly. "I'm leaving. The show was great. You looked amazing, baby. See you Monday at the office, okay?" He gave my lips a peck and sprinted towards Chad.

I entered the dimly lit room and found Blake standing in the center of it, eyes staring blankly at a portrait of Troy and me. "Blake?" I touched his arm lightly. He took a hold of my arm and linked it to his, lightly tugging me, making me follow him out of the room. *Don't panic. We'll work it out. He said he loved me. He did, didn't he? So, why hasn't he said it again?*

Instead of turning right to go back to the main room, he kept going forward to where I presumed the offices were located. He dragged me to the last one on the right. Opening the door, he flicked the switch, closed the door and locked it. It was a decent sized office with a big desk and a leather couch sitting across from it with a coffee table that had magazines splayed neatly across.

I turned around to face him and saw he was leaning against the gray door, eyes closed, hands in his pocket and his nose flaring; a clear indicator that he was furious with me. *The portraits, of course.* I didn't want to argue about that. *I did it for Chad and I don't give a hoot if he's mad about it. I love him... I do, but he just can't bulldoze his way around me.*

"Sienna, this is not how I pictured my reunion with you after almost six weeks of not seeing each other. I'm being rotten, *I know*, but I'm being eaten alive with jealousy. I can't think or breathe without pain. Was that the man who took you home the same night when you started working for Kyle?"

"Yes..." I admitted in a soft whisper.

"Did anything happen with you and this man? *Anything* at all?"

I shook my head. "No, apart from the intimate poses, no. Not in that sense."

His eyes fluttered open; the intensity of liquid silver dominated his midnight blue eyes, the usual gold flecks gone. The constant shift of his eye color depended on his mood and I was frozen in awe. He was compellingly riveting and spellbinding to those around him. *Does he know the kind of power he has with his looks alone? Does he know he can make me fall at his feet with a smile? Or is it the fact that he can slice me in two with a mere glance?*

"Are you attracted to him?"

Am I? I swallowed. He is hot, but enough to tempt me away from Blake? No, I didn't think there's a man out there who could. "Yes, he's good looking. Am I tempted? No. I only want you, Blake. I've only ever wanted you from the moment you kissed me. There's only one you and I'm not going to jeopardize us over asinine curiosity."

He moved past me and leaned slightly against the mahogany desk. "Come here," Blake commanded in a soft voice, but with an edge of something I couldn't pinpoint at the time. I did as he asked and stood before him, however he didn't even try to touch me. "Show me I'm the only one. *Prove it.*"

Prove it, he said. "Fine" and I would. I had been aching for him. If playing charades would get him to be inside me, then who was I to decline his request?

Slowly unbuckling his belt and his pants, I pulled his boxer briefs down all the way to his ankles. When his cock sprung free from the confines of his briefs, my insides melted from the sight of it and a flow of liquid oozed freely from my pussy. I knelt before him and took him in my mouth. His sharp indrawn of breath pleased me. I sucked his shaft all the way to the back of my throat and back out again; all the way to his engorged head, repeatedly.

His large hand pulled my hair and he rasped for me to stop. He commanded me to prop my elbows on the desk and to spread my legs open. I did. I felt him behind me as he pulled the ends of my dress and hiked it all the way above my butt. His finger traced the outline of the soft lace that covered my ass and then all the way to the front where he rubbed furiously.

"*You only get wet for me, Sienna?*" His tone told me he was still angry.

"*Only* you, Blake," I croaked as his finger drove me insane, my mind totally incapable of thinking.

"Are you lying to me?" *What the fuck?* How many times did I have to tell this infuriating man?

"Why the hell would I lie to you? There's no one else I want more than *you.*" It was so difficult to concentrate when his finger wouldn't stop rubbing me. I was trying with all my might to get it together.

A harsh sound came from him as he ripped my thong in two and flung it to the floor. He didn't tease his engorged head on my opening like he usually did; he just inserted himself with one powerful thrust and growled, "*Santo Cielo!* I've been dreaming about your silk tightness for so long. Forgive me if I can't control myself. God help me, but I can't stop wanting you." He held my hips tighter and pounded me very hard. His force was titillating and I lifted my ass more so that he could get his fill. My invitation was awarded with another growl. He lifted me so we were both on our feet as he cupped my breasts and used them to fuck me harder.

"*Baby... you feel so good... don't stop...*" I said in between moans. He bit the spot where my shoulder and neck connected. I yelped from the searing pain his teeth caused.

Blake pulled out and swiftly placed my limp body on the wide mahogany desk. Hooking my legs around his hips, he plunged inside me again. I couldn't take my eyes off him. He was watching his cock pummel me and I had never seen a sexier look on his face. I groaned as he shifted his position and picked up his pace to a grinding speed.

"I only want you... only you..." I panted, out of breath.

His hands held my shoulders and both of his thumbs pressed firmly on my throat. His dominating position made the effect of his fucking even more powerful. "You belong to me. I'm taking what's mine." The pressure on my throat and the pressure from my groin put together simply combusted me. Multiple-orgasms quaked and vibrated my entire body as he poured his seed in my womb.

Blake pulled me gently to him as he placed a gentle kiss on my lips. "Thank you, my love. I needed that," said as he heavily panted against me.

You can have me that way anytime. That was the best sex ever! Ever!

I lovingly smiled at him. "No, *thank you!* I love it when you're rough and unhinged. I enjoyed every second of it."

"Good to know because that was only the appetizer. I have more coming your way tonight." He gave me a wicked smile and at that moment, my heart convulsed with love.

I love you...

"Sounds like a plan, but for now, we have to get back before our friends start a search party for us."

I picked my ripped underwear up off the floor and was about to throw them in the waste bin when he took the decimated cloth from my hand. He bunched it up and placed it under his nose, inhaling my lingering scent.

Oh. My. Goodness.

His dazzling god-like smile in place, he shoved my torn underwear in his breast pocket. "Just a token of this eventful night, *amore.*" His toe-curling voice made me want to jump on him, but instead, I settled on his lips.

Amore, he said.

Love.

The man did speak five languages, fluently.

Thirty-two

We'd been seeing each other daily. Today was Thursday and he'd be leaving again Sunday. Long distance with Blake was such a bummer and since he was leaving soon, I'd decided to surprise him at one of the corporate offices in South Bank.

The idea came when I was walking out of my last class of the day. It was only three in the afternoon and I didn't feel like going home early so I hailed a passing cab. The high-rise glass building was magnificent.

I eyed the automatic glass door wearily. I wasn't exactly dressed appropriately for office visits. It was nearing the end of August and the weather had been chilly for the last few days, but today, the weather greeted me with warm rays of sunshine and I succumbed to the impulse of wearing this outfit. I was wearing a well-worn, short, denim skirt, white cami and dark brown cowboy boots with my hair down, finishing my look; a look of a college student no doubt. *Oh well, whatever. I want to see him; who cares what people think?* I didn't wear much make-up today. Well, I didn't usually do much when I go to school. All I needed was tinted moisturizer, a dab of gloss and a few swipes of mascara.

Should I call him first? Maybe not. I wanted to surprise him. I was sure he was going be delighted to see me. Blake had been insatiable ever since he'd landed Saturday from New York.

Feeling optimistic, I strolled to the entrance. It was all glass and black marble tiles with a touch of chrome around the bank of elevators at the far-end of the building. I stopped and greeted one of the polished pretty receptionists; there were six of them. "Hello, I'm here to see Blake Knightly. Can you direct me to his office?" She stopped typing on her white Apple computer and glanced in my direction. The auburn hair, blue-eyed woman gave me a cold stare and mocked my outfit with her eyes. She almost laughed at me, but managed to stifle it. *Catty much?*

"And *who* might you be? Do you have an appointment?" Her condescending attitude continued.

"I'm Sienna Richards. I don't have an appointment. This was a spur of the moment kind of thing. I'm one of his close friends."

"*Sure you are.* Give me a minute." With a few clicks, she spoke into her tiny headpiece and started typing. After a couple of minutes—but what felt like forever—she handed me a keycard pass with my name and pointed to the set of elevators. She instructed me to swipe the keycard on the scanner and it would take me to Blake's floor.

Her forced smile made me leave the reception area without even saying thanks. She certainly didn't deserve one. *Is that how they receive guests here? It's pretty scary.* It was worse than going to the dentist.

I was about to step inside one of the elevators when a woman stopped and faced me with a hateful smirk. I froze. It was the woman from the text message. The picture hadn't done her beauty justice. She was even more striking in person.

"*Yes?*" Here I was, hoping my frosty attitude would send her away.

"You should stop this chasing that you're doing, *querida*. You will get hurt and you seem like a nice, pretty little girl." Her Spanish accent was evident.

"I'm not chasing anyone. I'm here to see my boyfriend. So, if you please, could you move out of my fucking way, *bruja!*" *Hag.*

The woman laughed like she had all the time in her little, whimsical world. She even had the gall to look amused. She was a bitch with a capital B. "You are a little spitfire, aren't you? No wonder my dear Blake can't get enough. He always loves it rough, wouldn't you say? But he won't be yours for long." Her wide, bitch smile was in place. "In less than four months, he'll be officially engaged, my dear." *Engaged? Blake? No, it can't be.* This woman was bluffing and plotting because she wanted Blake all to herself.

"Engaged to whom? Y*ou?* Right, like I would believe anything that comes out of that salacious, poisonous mouth of yours." *What a lowlife. Doesn't she have anything else to do besides spewing lies and pestering others?* She chuckled again in her stupid, annoying laugh. I was seriously tempted to punch the twilights out of her, but I didn't want to make a scene.

The women looked thoughtful for a moment before she spat her venom at me. "How I wish it was me. Papa and mama love him. The lucky lady was Camilla Clayworth. He's been engaged since he was eighteen. He didn't tell you, did he? Well, that's too bad. Well, it was great to meet you. Good luck!" She sauntered past me like she was up for Miss Universe. *Is it true? Is Blake really engaged? He never said anything. Well duh. Start moving and ask the man himself.*

I did as instructed and scanned the keycard with a shaky hand and the elevator came to life. Floor after floor I went up. The light indicator on the panel was finally on the last floor before the 'P.' I was assuming that it stood for penthouse.

With a silent swoosh of the elevator doors I stepped out onto the carpeted floor. There was another model-type, blonde receptionist behind a desk. *Do all the receptionists in this building look like they just stepped out of Vogue? What kind of a discriminatory workplace is this? A very pretty one. It's a no brainer why men in suits gawk and pant with all these hot women around all day at work wearing tight-fitting suits. It was no wonder lawsuits are quite common in this arena.*

"Ms. Richards? I'm Larissa. Why don't you take a seat while I page Luke? He should be here shortly to get you."

Murmuring my thanks, I turned and sat in one of the lounge chairs. I was surprised she wasn't hostile like the other hellcat in the lobby. Frankly, I was ready for another battle. *I might get my wish if this farcical innuendo turns out to be true.* I wasn't naïve enough to think that arranged marriages were abolished back in the medieval period. These things were quite common with the blue-blooded, upper-crust society. And Blake was one of them. I was sure his lineage could be traced as far back as before Christ.

Luke came to greet me before my butt had time to warm the seat cushion. He genuinely seemed happy to see me, but his mood didn't rub off on me. I was polite, but obviously it was strained. Who wouldn't be, given the situation?

"He's just finishing up a call, but he should be done soon." He opened a dark cherry oak door and I thanked him graciously.

Blake's office overlooked the River Thames and his executive black desk sat right in the middle of the room. He was on a call, but looked up when I entered and gave me one of his signature dashing smiles. I lamely waved back and strolled over to the far right floor-to-ceiling glass window and gloomily stared at the view below me. I was nervous and I had no idea how to bring the subject up. He looked happy to see me.

If he is engaged... then I have to walk away. The big question is, can I leave him? Blake had become my life. I lived and breathed him. My love for him was so much more than the kind I had felt for Kyle. Blake consumed my soul.

I was so engrossed in my own thoughts that I didn't hear him coming. I was jolted back into reality when I felt his arms wrap around my waist. He kissed and nuzzled my neck before speaking. "When you walked through the door, I was just thinking about you. It's a good thing we read each other's minds so well."

Tilting my head so he could kiss me, I sighed with a heavy heart when our lips made contact. I kissed him like it was the last time. I kissed with my heart.

"Babe, can we talk?" My stern voice broke the spell.

"That sounds ominous. Why don't we go and sit, shall we?" He guided me towards the other section of the room where there was a sectional couch and a bar of refreshments. Neither of us sat on it. I stood behind one of the lounge chairs, anxious. He leaned against the bar and folded his arms.

"What is it? You're being odd."

"Are you—by any chance—engaged?" He froze in shock. His face horrified. *Oh, fuck!*

"Where did you get this information?"

"From a relevant source. Be honest with me. Is. It. True?"

He exhaled a defeated sigh and weaved a hand through his hair as his other hand squeezed the bridge of his nose. "A day before I turned eighteen, my grandfather summoned me to his study. He told me that the Clayworth wanted me to marry their daughter, Camilla. When he broke the news, I wasn't at all surprised. The Clayworths were very good friends with my parents. I grew up with Camilla and it was always spoken between our families that they wished it, when the time came. Camilla's lovely and I didn't have any qualms about being married to her, so I said yes with one condition. The condition was for them to wait until I was at the age of twenty-five. I didn't mean for you to find out this way; I'm so very sorry."

"Have you had sex with her?"

"She lost her virginity to me and on occasion, we would meet up and go somewhere for vacation. It's been our tradition ever since the agreement. It was our way of getting to know each other."

"You weren't planning to tell me, huh? I'm just your little plaything on the side until you get married. I'm a quick fuck for you. I get it. I see everything clearly now."

He rushed to my side and tried to hold my hand, but I bunched them together until they were white. I couldn't stand to be touched by him. "No, Sienna, it wasn't like that at all. I wanted you from the first moment. You've been my friend; don't do this. I'll fix it. I'll talk to the Clayworths."

"You are a liar. One of the things I asked of you is your honesty and yet from the very beginning, you were lying. How many women have you fucked while being with me? God! I'm so stupid!"

"I haven't had anyone, except for you."

"Right, like I should believe what comes out of those lying lips? Forget you. I'm done. Don't contact me because I'm through with you."

I was about to reach for the door when he held me down with his arms, wrapping my body like steel. "I'm sorry. I'll figure a way out; don't leave. I love you. I've been in love with you for a long time. Don't do this to us." I fought against his hold and he finally released me.

"HOW FUCKING DARE YOU! *You love me?* This is how you show you love someone?" my tears started falling freely. "The pain I feel right now—it's a hundred times worse than what Kyle ever did to me. This is your *love?* Well, I DO NOT WANT IT! Give it to your fiancée. I'm sure she'll gladly take it, you lying sack of shit! I regret the day I let you in my life!" with that, I left and ran to the elevator.

My heart was beating frantically.

I didn't feel relieved until I was in the safety of a cab.

Thirty-three

I was still in a state of shock. The whole scene flashed vividly in my mind. I ordered the driver to take me to a place where I could find some solace. I didn't want to be bothered with questions at home from Lucy.

I paid the cab driver and entered the house with my key. I was on autopilot as I headed for the stairs. When I reached the top, I saw Kyle come out of his bedroom. His huge grin turned into a questioning frown as he got closer.

"Sienna, what's wrong? What happened?" My knees buckled and Kyle caught me before I landed on the wooden floor.

"He's engaged, Kyle. I've fallen in love with a guy who's promised to someone else." I started to laugh hysterically at the situation. I reluctantly followed my heart and look where that left me. The dream of having Blake in my life—waking up next to him and seeing him smile lovingly at me—was gone. All gone and soon he'd be doing all those things with the wretched Camilla. That image hit me quite literally. I howled from the pain. I cried, like how I cried when I found out my dad had died.

Kyle held me until I stopped sobbing with my pain and gently carried me to his bed, covering my body with a comforter. He didn't even bother taking my shoes off. He placed himself on top of the comforter and held me as I cried myself into unconsciousness.

I woke up later feeling like I had drowned and been brought back to life. I checked the clock on the side table, five thirty-six a.m. I felt Kyle still holding me. Bless him, he never asked about what happened. It was always like that with him. I liked how he never asked and always waited for me to initiate it.

I was just about to slide off the bed when he stirred. "Hey, why don't you wash up and I'll make some breakfast? You didn't eat last night. You have to eat something."

Pursing my lips, I nodded. "Okay, let me just wash my face and brush my teeth then I'll come down."

Padding my way to the bathroom, I looked for a spare toothbrush and found one in the very last drawer. I didn't even bother checking what my face looked like. I knew my eyes were red and swollen. I just couldn't bear seeing it and looking myself in the eye. I just might have had a nervous breakdown.

After washing up, I took a scrunchy from my purse and tied my hair up then I headed downstairs, barefoot and in my same clothes from yesterday. *Kyle probably took my shoes off in the middle of the night.* I sighed.

I found him making two cups of coffee. There were two plates with ham and cheese omelets on the breakfast table. I took a seat as he placed a hot, freshly brewed coffee next to me. "Thank you, Kyle, but you didn't have to wake up this early and make me breakfast."

"You're talking crazy. That was nothing compared to your usual crazy PMS days."

I smiled. "Geez, why do you always bring that up? Either way; thank you." I took a huge sip of my coffee and a hefty bite of the omelet.

We were silent for a while until he spoke, "I'm actually leaving for Heathrow to go back to LA today, for two weeks. My flight's at ten-thirty. So I had to wake up anyway."

I paused. *He was leaving for two weeks?* "You never said. Why didn't you say anything?"

"You've been busy with Blake since Saturday and I didn't want to bother you. It was irrelevant."

"How can that be irrelevant? You should've told me at least. I would've showed up at work Friday and found you gone. What the hell?"

Kyle shrugged. "I honestly didn't think it was a big deal. I just didn't want to bother you, 'kay?"

"Well, we're best friends. You should tell me every time you plan to leave the country. I worry, too."

"Fine, okay. I'll do that if it makes you happy."

I murmured thank you and took another sip of my coffee. I didn't have much of an appetite and I had to force myself to eat. Kyle wouldn't have it if I didn't eat and I couldn't deal with another argument at that point.

Blake... was he hurting, too? Maybe, maybe not. I didn't know him anymore. I thought I had, but that simply wasn't the case. That mask he put on sometimes never came off. I never knew which one I'd get when I was with him. He could be deceiving. I had been dangerously playing with fire and I had gotten burnt.

Kyle took both of our plates to the sink and cleaned up. I got up and sat on one of the stools that faced him. "Hey, I was thinking... would you mind if I go home with you? I don't want to stay here. I just want to get away for a bit. I can email my teachers and tell them that there's an emergency back home."

"*You sure?* You're not going to get in trouble? I know you're hurting, baby, but you can't mess up school. You've worked so hard to get here; don't mess it up. But, if your teachers are going to be okay with it, then who am I to stop you?" I went over to his side and gave him a big hug.

"Thank you! Thank you! Now, I have to go and pack. I don't want to miss our flight."

He called me a cab and we agreed that it would be easier for him to pick me up from the flat and we'd head to the airport from there. He'd pick me up around seven-thirty and it was already quarter past six. I technically had an hour to shower and pack.

The idea of going home with him came out of nowhere, but I was glad I thought of it because I couldn't stand staying here after the break-up. The thought of seeing Blake terrified me. The idea of seeing him with someone else so soon was definitely going to kill me. I knew I was running away from it all, but I wasn't strong enough to face any of my friends and explain the situation.

Thirty-four

The ride from Kyle's house in Hampstead to Covent Garden took half the time than usual without traffic. I graciously thanked the driver and hurriedly entered the building. I quietly made my way into the apartment, not wanting to wake Lucy out of her sleep. I hunted for my luggage, unzipped it and lugged it onto the bed. I couldn't even look at the bed without seeing images of Blake and me making love on it.

Shit, this is going to be difficult.

I felt like I was a walking, breathing dead person. There was a heavy-knotted feeling on my chest. Every time I breathed it hurt. It felt like someone had jammed my heart with a knife, pulled it out and left me open and bleeding.

I started taking off my clothes when I heard a knock on my door. I froze. *Shit, is that Blake?*

"May I come in?" Lucy's soft voice said against the door.

"Yep, come on in," I answered.

She walked in the room looking half awake and her eyes widened when she saw the luggage on my bed. "Where are you going?"

"I'm going back home with Kyle for a couple of weeks. I *need* some space... away."

She sighed and sat next to my luggage. "Blake's been calling my phone every hour checking if you came home. He's going barmy and acting like a nutter. Haven't you checked your phone?" I shook my head. I didn't dare check it.

"Listen, I don't know why you guys broke up and I feel awful that you guys did; I love you both and I hate that it's come to this. He didn't want to talk about the reason why you guys did. Would it be okay if I tell him that you're home and you're safe? The man hasn't slept because he's been so worried."

"Yeah, that's fine," my small voice croaked a response. She got up and hugged me.

"If going back home will help, then go, but if you're not sure, then best you fix it with him; if there's a chance for you both. Just think about it, okay? I love you, my dear friend. I'll let Chad know later on today. Don't forget to let us know that you've arrived safely, all right?" She kissed my cheek and quietly left the room.

My eyes burned, but no tears formed. I guess I had run out of tears from all the excessive crying I had done last night. I jumped in the shower for ten minutes and got out to change.

Was there anything to contemplate with Blake? He lied. Technically, he hid the truth. He didn't man up and confess his little dirty secret. *Is the engagement his dirty little secret or I am? Now that I think about it, he never once asked me to accompany him to any of the events or galas he attended. Apart from our friends, he never invited me to meet other people he dealt business with.*

Fuck, this realization hurts. I had always wondered, but I didn't dwell on it because I was just happy being with him. I didn't need all the bells and whistles. I only wanted him and I didn't care about all the lavish parties he went to. The joke was on me. He only used me for sex. His declaration of love was pure bullshit.

I hastily changed into black, stretchy-skinny jeans and a black, fitted shirt with black, wedge heels. I pulled my wet hair in a bun and rummaged through my closet and my essential toiletries. I jammed them all in the luggage without a care. I didn't even bother with make-up and settled for sheer lip-gloss instead. *Kyle should be here in five minutes. I had better get moving so I can meet him downstairs.*

I found Luce in the kitchen, drinking her morning coffee. Poor thing, she looked like hell from lack of sleep. Blake was so inconsiderate to bother Lucy in the middle of the night like a psycho. I knew he was worried, but Luce needed her sleep. Her school was taking up a lot of her time as it was. I hated Blake even more when I got a glimpse of her dark circles. We said our quick goodbyes and I left for downstairs.

Dragging my luggage out of the elevator and straight out of the main door, I didn't see the person waiting for me. "*Sienna, please talk to me.* I've been out of my wits with worry since last night when you didn't come home." His eyes spied my luggage. "Going on a trip?"

"Yes, in fact, Kyle should be here any second. He's going back home for a while and I invited myself along."

"Why would you do that? You know how I feel about him. He's in love with you! He's going to take this opportunity and turn it in his favor."

"That would certainly be up to me, don't you think? Stop wasting your time."

"No, we can figure it out. I don't want to be with anyone else. I love you, Sienna, with everything that I am. I love you." *Liar, if he did... he would've ended his engagement before I even found out, but he didn't.*

He raked a hand through his hair. Dammit, he looks beautiful and sexy as hell.

"Stop lying to yourself and *to me*. Game over, so you should drop the act—" He swiftly captured my lips and I reeled from the impact of his kiss. After a few times of trying to coax my lips into submission, I gave in to my lecherous body. *God, kissing him feels perfect... it feels like home.*

I love him so much, it hurts. My tears fell freely and we both tasted them, but he didn't stop. With a deep, heavy, guttural growl, he pulled my lips away and cradled my cheeks with his hands. "Did that feel like a game to you?" I lowered my eyes and stared at his chest. "*Damn you!* That kiss felt more real than anything else in this world. You love me! That kiss just proved that you do. I love you, too, Sienna. I can't live without you... will you marry me?"

I gasped and stared at him like a deer caught in the headlights as he got on a bended knee. He produced a ginormous rock. It was certainly more than fifteen carats. The ring was a princess-cut, canary diamond surrounded with smaller diamonds and had been designed in a halo pattern with diamonds surrounding the entire band; the eternity band.

"The color of the rock reminds me of the color of your eyes when they get caught with the sun, like liquid gold. I commissioned this ring to be made the day after I left for New York. That night, I knew you were *it* for me. I don't want anyone else. I know everything's been unfolding so quickly, but I wanted—needed—you to know how much you mean to me. *I love you wholeheartedly.* Will you please let me be the happiest man in all of England and say *yes*?"

I stared wide-eyed at the ring, back to his face and back to the ring again. Shocked didn't even begin to cover my reaction.

"Blake... I'm sorry... I can't."

He abruptly stood up and grabbed my face with a fierce scowl. "What do you mean you can't? How hard is it to say yes?"

"I can't. I'm sorry," I stammered through my tears.

"I see. I guess, I imagined that you felt the same way, but I suppose that's all it was, all in my imagination."

He heaved and turned to me with a stony face. "You'll regret this because I've only ever loved you and when you see me happy with another woman, you'll regret it even more. Your thoughts will be haunted by me; the one that got away. Goodbye, Sienna." He stood there for a few seconds before sliding in the Aston Martin, gunning the engine and rapidly vanishing through the traffic.

I wiped away my tears and exhaled a long sigh. I had done the right thing, I knew I had. *He lied. I can't trust him!*

Kyle's cologne penetrated the air, letting me know that he was close to me. "Did you see all of that?"

"I did. Sienna, you love him. And it hurts for me to say this, but what if you're making a mistake? Don't you think you should give it another shot?"

What good would it be without trust? It was worthless without trust.

How can one be happy with a liar? One who keeps secrets such as having a fucking fiancée? Even if I did give him another chance, I would be permanently living in a state of paranoia. I couldn't do that to myself.

I did the right thing; the best thing. It might not feel like it now, but it would be in the long run.

"No, let's leave it at that. We have to get going. I don't want to miss the flight."

~S~

I didn't let my thoughts wander to Blake's proposal until I was seated. I ached while I watched the fluffy, white clouds through the airplane window as I listened to "Lovesong" by Adele from my iPod.

What happened today was life changing for me. I didn't know if I would be able to get over it. The hurt and pain was rooted deeply inside of me. I didn't doubt that I would see him again; we did have common friends. It was simply inevitable.

I may be broken right now, but the next time I set foot in London, I would be a different woman. A much stronger one, I hoped.

One that men didn't trample on.

Chasing Imperfection
Out Now
Chasing Paradise
July 2013

OTHER BOOKS BY THE AUTHOR:
Scornfully Yours (Torn Series)
Frayed (Torn Series)
Scorned (Torn Series)
Scornfully Hers (Torn Series)
Blasphemous (Torn Series)
Lily's Mistake

Coming Soon:

Falling For My Husband
Loving Lily (Lily's Mistake)
My Summer in Venice
Pieces of You & Me
Undeniably Yours (Torn Series)
Fixated On You (Torn Series)

Acknowledgements:

I just want to say thanks to my family and friends who have pushed me to write and for being there to support me through it all. THANK YOU!

To my mom, thank you for being a constant rock through my ups and downs and always encouraging me to follow my dreams. You're the best! And I'm lucky to have a mom like you.

To all the readers, thank you for all the love and support. I greatly appreciate it!!!!

http://pamelaannbooks.blogspot.com

You can follow me here:
http://www.facebook.com/pamela.annauthor
https://twitter.com/PamelaAnnAuthor

Printed in Great Britain
by Amazon.co.uk, Ltd.,
Marston Gate.